The Deserters

A NOVEL

Pamela Mulloy

ESPLANADE BOOKS

THE FICTION IMPRINT AT VÉHICULE PRESS

ESPLANADE BOOKS IS THE FICTION IMPRINT AT VÉHICULE PRESS

Published with the generous assistance of the Canada Council for
the Arts and the Canada Book Fund of the Department
of Canadian Heritage.

Funded by the Government of Canada
Financé par le gouvernement du Canada | **Canadä**

Esplanade Books editor: Dimitri Nasrallah
Cover design: David Drummond
Photo of author: Ayelet Tsabari
Typeset in Minion and Filosofia
Printed by Marquis Printing Inc.

LIBRARY AND ARCHIVES CANADA CATALOGUING IN PUBLICATION

Mulloy, Pamela, 1961-, author
The deserters / Pamela Mulloy.

Issued in print and electronic formats.
ISBN 978-1-55065-495-0 (softcover) – ISBN 978-1-55065-502-5 (HTML)

I. Title.

PS8626.U465D47 2018   C813'.6   C2018-900679-X
C2018-900680-3

Published by Véhicule Press, Montréal, Québec, Canada
vehiculepress.com

Distribution in Canada by LitDistCo
www.litdistco.ca

Distribution in the U.S. by Independent Publishers Group
www.ipgbook.com

Printed in Canada on FSC® certified paper.

For Darren and for Esme

These are the days that really belong to the moon.

—MICHAEL ONDAATJE, *In the Skin of a Lion*

So must I be called of no account and a coward
if I must carry out every order you may happen
to give me.

Tell other men to do these things, but give me
no more commands, since I for my part have no
intention to obey you...

—*The Iliad*

Spring

THE FARMHOUSE SHOULD HAVE BEEN ABANDONED. The clapboard shingles, ashen from gnawing weather, windows cracked or broken. The house sagged, mourned the passing of time. Dean was drawn to its angular structure, its gables, a high-pitched roof, its elegance. It was a perfect place to assume squatter's rights.

He'd been watching the place, off and on, for two days and was ready to stake his claim. Then, early on the third day, he saw her emerging from the kitchen, her nightdress flapping around her knees.

It was a milky spring morning, the grass laden with dew. A lingering fog gave the place a feeling of neglect, and so her presence added to the dreamlike quality that led him to think he could live here. Through the crack in the barn door, he listened for sounds: another voice, a dog barking, doors closing. But there was nothing.

A blue jay squawked as it flew past, an unwelcome informer.

Crouched on the straw floor, the dust compelled Dean to sneeze. He suppressed it so there was hardly a sound, then peered through the opening again, waiting. It seemed that waiting was all he ever did any more.

The woman gazed out across the yard. She rubbed her face and pushed her thick black hair away from her eyes. She moved like a child, though Dean figured she'd seen forty already. She wore a chunky wool sweater over a nightdress that lay shapeless against her, so that she looked hidden beneath a pile of clothes, her pale thin legs out of proportion with the mass of garments that protected her from the morning chill. Her eyes swept the property lazily, not really seeing, just looking. When her gaze fell upon the barn door where he stood, he dared not breathe. Then she moved on, and he exhaled slowly.

It seemed to him that she was crazy, staring blandly into the day like that. Barely moving, sipping her coffee. All the while, he acted like he was back on a surveillance mission, feeling captive, waiting for her to go inside so he could escape. She stood there a good long time, taking in the day before retreating back into the house.

This happened every morning for the next three days, him sneaking his way into the barn before she got up, waiting for her to come out, watching her soak in the morning, and then returning to camp.

∾

Eugenie caught a glimpse of him as he came over the top of the hill. His loping gait and swinging arms, a man of singular purpose. She immediately thought he was delivering bad news: a neighbour's complaint, unpaid taxes, someone dead. She took a few steps towards him then stopped and leaned against the spade. She thought to pick up the scattering of tools that lay by her feet, but she didn't know how that would help the situation. So she waited.

"Your rows are going the wrong way." He gestured towards the garden she'd just finished laying out.

She was unused to company, especially a stranger walking

onto her property without notice. For a moment, she considered telling him to get off her land. "How so?" she asked finally.

"A good rain will carry the soil down the troughs and you'll have a pile of mud at the bottom. If you run the rows parallel to the river, the rain water gets trapped between them, then the ground gets a good soaking and you don't get a mud slide."

Eugenie looked at him, then at the rows that suddenly seemed awkward in their perpendicular location, not in rhythm with river or slope.

"It won't take much to reposition them. I can help, if you're interested."

Eugenie looked at the garden again. All that hard work, wasted. One more setback. She stood chewing at a nail, concentrating on her failure.

"I'm looking for work. Neil Ferguson said you might have something."

"Oh. I see. I'll speak to my husband."

Dean hesitated, said he'd come back another day and strode up the hill. Eugenie turned and watched him go, at once weary with the weight of the task upon her. It had taken her two days to set out the rows; the idea of doing it again defeated her.

"You know," she called out. "Maybe I can use your help in the garden. Then we'll see if there's anything else for you."

"Sure," he shrugged.

She saw his face loosen. He was younger than her by a few years. As she watched him walk back toward the garden, she saw creases in his face that marked him as someone used to outdoor work.

"Maybe on the workshop roof, or the new orchard," she said, thinking out loud.

"Sure."

"Eugenie Waters." She held out her hand.

"Dean," he said, his handshake too rough for her light grasp. "I'll get started."

Dean took the spade from her. He walked up and down the garden, considering where to begin, then went to one corner and sliced the spade into the dirt. His movements swift and vigorous, he worked his way along the top of the slope until he had cut the tops off each row and formed a new one in the other direction.

While he dug, Eugenie worked her way along the newly formed rows, smoothing out the pebbled soil along the ridged lines, gently nudging the dirt into shape with the back of her rake. The scrape and slice of their implements negated any need for conversation, forming an antiquated rhythm, like farm machinery. Their enterprise pushed Eugenie until her arms ached.

"They'll think I'm mad," Eugenie said when they finally stopped for a break. She gestured to the farm across the river, the growl of the tractor calling their attention. "First one way, then another. They'll wonder what I'm up to."

"I wouldn't worry what they think," Dean said, lighting a cigarette.

She wiped her face with a handkerchief, then pulled an orange from her sack.

"Are you from around here?" Eugenie asked, peeling the orange.

"Not really," he replied.

"We moved from England a year ago," she said, after it became clear he would offer no further information. "My husband is in Spain. He'll be returning soon." She held out sections of

14

the orange in her hand. "Would you like some?" He was already reaching for the spade, but paused to accept her offer. He ate them eagerly, with an urgency that caused her to reach back in her bag and give him half a sandwich.

"It's a lot of work for one person," he said between bites.

"Michael will be able to help when he gets here," Eugenie said, tossing the orange rinds into the wheelbarrow. She wanted to say more about Michael, about their plans to set up the farm and how they'd been forestalled by Michael's work, how it had been two months since she'd seen her husband, and would likely be another three before he'd be back, but Dean had finished his sandwich and was already off to start another row on the far side of the garden. She wiped her hands on her shirtsleeves, picked up her rake and went over to join him.

The wind blew along the river valley in swirls and puffs. The threat of an afternoon storm hung in the air. With faces flushed and a sense of urgency driving them, they finished preparing the garden just as a few bulging raindrops began to fall, and then rushed up the hill, she pushing the wheelbarrow of tools while he shouldered the spades.

"Come in for a cold drink," she said, dumping the tools in the barn.

Eugenie entered her kitchen, suddenly aware that she'd not had any company for weeks. The newspaper sprawled across the kitchen table, the cutting board covered in the morning's crumbs, dishes by the sink. This is what living alone had done. She'd forgotten the few simple niceties one needs to keep the house orderly, to live orderly. She took a few long strides to the table and half rolled, half folded the paper and set it near the wood stove. She swept the crumbs off the breadboard with her hand and gave it a quick wipe before putting it back in the cupboard. She did this quickly with one eye to Dean who was outside having a cigarette. The kitchen had gone dim with the rain, the change in atmosphere giving her perspective on the situation, the fact that she was alone with a stranger. She glanced at the poker that stood near the wood stove.

Eugenie took two glasses of iced tea out to the porch. They stood looking outwards, judging the density of the rain.

Dean turned to examine the screen door, which slanted downward. "That needs to be re-hung."

"There's a lot to do here."

Eugenie looked at him, wanting to tell him that she'd planned to paint the kitchen, clear out the attic and get the cold cellar ready for the canning she was intending to do in the coming months. But she was having a hard time getting started, couldn't explain why she lacked the motivation. She went back inside to a piece of paper pinned to the wall, peered at the smudged list, and settled on its third item.

"How are you with fences?" she called through the screen door.

"Fences?"

"We don't have any animals to keep in, but we should try to keep the undesirables out." She stepped back out onto the porch. "A place with broken down fences looks bad."

"That's true enough."

"It's stopped raining," she said. They walked out into the yard. "Do you live nearby?"

"Not far. I'm staying at my uncle's camp."

They were out in the centre of the yard, the farm buildings forming a circle around them, the sound of a car on the road a distant reminder that there were others who occupied these parts. She snuck a sideways glance at him, wishing he would say more about himself. The stiffness that had focussed his efforts to complete the garden now made her feel awkward as she showed him around the yard.

"That's the garage, where you should find the tools you need. There's the old granary, the workshop, the barn, which is used mostly for storage now." As she pulled open the barn door, she heard the telephone from inside the house. "I'd better get that. I'll be right back."

Eugenie ran inside, thinking it was Michael. She was anxious to tell him about Dean and the plans she had. Michael had been distracted in his own way these days. He'd put off coming to Canada three times in as many months. He kept getting new commissions; his apprenticeship with Antonio was finally paying off.

"Michael." Eugenie was breathless by the time she picked up the phone.

"Eugenie? No, it's me." It was Ivy, her sister.

Eugenie slumped down on the stool. "Where are you?"

"I'm in Montreal. How are things?"

She had not spoken to her sister since Ivy had returned from a teaching stint in Japan a month ago. "Busy," she sighed into the telephone.

"I've got some time coming up soon. I thought I'd come home for a bit to see you."

Eugenie closed her eyes, trying to think how she might ward off her sister's visit. "Sure, Ivy. You're always welcome. Be warned though. The place is still in rough shape."

"That's okay. I just need a break from the city."

"Just let me know when you're coming." Eugenie glanced out the window in search of Dean, only half-listening to her sister's plans. When she got off the phone she went back outside, but he was nowhere in sight. She called out to him as she walked from one building to the next, but it was clear he had gone. She searched the lane, the pathways, the fields that spread out from the farm, but there was no trace of him.

Finally, Eugenie closed the garage door and sat down on the bench outside. She held one hand out parallel to the horizon, lining her fingers up so they filled the gap between sun and land. Two fingers. Fifteen minutes of light for each finger meant that it would be dark in half an hour.

She stayed on the bench, feeling the day's aches jab at her body, until the waning light forced her up. Yearning for a bath, Eugenie eased herself toward the house when she spotted Dean's glass on the porch. Inside the glass was a scrap of paper. *Gone home. See you in the morning.* She slipped the note into her pocket and went into the house, securing both locks.

∾

Air whooshed past, followed by a shudder. Dean's body was vibrating. Another mortar attack: he squinted the dust from his eyes, scraping away dirt from his face. Logs splintered a few feet from him. Gunshots. Bullet after bullet, chewing at the wood, kicking up the rocks nearby. He pressed closer to the ground. Dirt in his nose, he fought to keep breathing. Then nothing. His heart banging. He squeezed his eyes shut, felt the dust coat his eyelids. His face ached. He ran his hand along the rubble, dragging gravel, feeling pebbles in his hand. Groping blindly.

18

Where the hell was his gun? Voices. He held his breath. They were getting closer. He let out a mournful wail, feeling it from somewhere deep inside.

The moan jolted Dean from another nightmare. Panting, he rushed out from his tent and stumbled around his camp, kicking over a can of beans he'd eaten for dinner the night before, splattering juice on his pant leg. He started running on the spot. One-two-three-four, one-two-three-four. When he thought he'd done a hundred, he slowed down, walked to the nearby brook and splashed water over his head. He splashed himself until his shirt was soaked. He tore open a granola bar and ate it in three bites, stripping off his shirt then using it to wipe the sweat from his armpits before dropping it into the water. He nudged it deeper with a stick, working it into an eddy where he left it to soak. Back at the tent, he reached into his pack for another shirt and put it on. Then a button broke free so he wrestled it off again, settling on a T-shirt.

Dean made it to the farm by eight. He walked past the house to survey the corner of the fence that needed fixing. He was cold so he walked briskly, flexing his hands as he went. He kicked at a fence post. It cracked easily, revealing the rotting wood. He kicked at it again so that it leaned heavily into the field. Then he went to the next post and kicked it until it too toppled, then the next and the next.

"Will you go on kicking all of my fence?" Eugenie called out. Dean swung around, startled that he hadn't heard her approach. She was walking holding out a coffee to him as she cradled her own against her chest for warmth.

"Here," he said, pulling off a piece of wood and handing it to her. "The undesirables have already eaten your fence away."

"What is it?"

"Carpenter ants, most likely. You'll need new posts, new fencing, and white gravel around to keep them out this time. We should replace these five here and another five up the lane. You'll need to go into town to get supplies." They stood examining the damage then worked out a plan.

Dean turned to the hole he'd started with the last rotten stump. "I'll give you a list. I'll stay here and dig the holes."

He was already digging his sixth hole when he watched her turn onto the road. He waited until she was out of sight before he dropped the spade and headed for the house.

∾

Eugenie had been at her bedroom window when Dean stepped through the sprawling bushes at the edge of the woods that morning, peering through curtains that barely concealed her. She saw him brush himself down, saw his arms swinging vigorously against the morning chill as he walked to the house.

It had been an hour since Michael's call, and she hadn't been able to fall back asleep.

"It's me," he'd whispered when she mumbled into the telephone. "Did I wake you?"

"I was just getting up." She rolled over and closed her eyes. "You okay?"

"I'm in the studio."

Eugenie pictured Michael sitting at his workbench, the whitewashed walls filled with sketches and photographs of marquetry and furniture designs, notes pinned to the lamp clamped to the table. Their house in Spain was near the top of the village and Michael's workshop even higher, along a goat path that led to the shed he'd bought from a farmer when they'd moved there. He'd had windows put in to offer natural light, shutters to keep the heat out, and electricity so that he was able to work late into the night.

"How is your work going?"

"Better."

"Oh?"

"I had a few glitches. I'm still trying to work them out."

Eugenie was silent for a moment. She lay back on her pillow and watched the curtain ripple in the breeze. She thought of Conchar and what it would be like to be there now, with Michael. It seemed too long since they'd been together, she was losing the memory of his touch. The time spent in the village that lay crouched in the mountains near the Alpujarras, faint traces of lemon in the air, the almond trees, the olive groves, seemed a portal away from the life she now led. More than once it occurred to her that they should never have moved to such a place, a place that could capture Michael's imagination and leave her outside it all.

"Michael?"

"Yes."

"When are you coming back?"

In his second of hesitation she heard a rush of water in the background that marked the irrigation system of the Spanish village. She closed her eyes to isolate the sound, like a dam unleashed. Day and night, a gate opened somewhere in the village, dictated by a rigid timetable, the water rushing to one garden, then the lock shutting down and the water rerouted to the next. They had been charmed in those early days, sitting out on the grassy ledge, their only outdoor space. They'd bring out a bottle of wine, their books, perhaps a game to pass the time. Their bare feet resting in wild thyme, the view of the Sierra Nevada mountains in the distance, and the water, funnelling here and there every half hour according to a system that seemed both antiquated and environmentally sound.

Now, with the burst of water lengthening the silence, she no longer wished to be in Conchar, with its impossible twisting roads leading to the entrance of the village, the constant climbing and descending as they made their way through the streets, even their house, built into a cave that backed into the mountain, the bathroom wall chiselled from rock, was more a place with potential, the plans to renovate it remaining on the drawing board.

He detailed for her some supplies he needed to locate and then asked quickly about the farm.

"Michael, when will you be coming home?" she repeated.

"Soon, my love. Soon."

The assurance that he would soon be there had kept her steady these past months, allowed her to continue to work on the place as if nothing was wrong. The winter had taken its toll, she knew. Her nerves were frayed. She kept telling herself that it was just a temporary situation, but somehow that didn't make up for endless nights when silence threatened to drive her mad. If she could keep thinking logically, acting rationally, she would manage.

Hiring Dean was a start. She had to keep a hold on things. It was not just the wind whistling through the cracks, the smoking stove, the creaks and moans of a house that had survived more than a hundred winters but had been left to rot the last five. There was more to the place than that, and Michael knew it when he convinced her they should take up the place, make a go of it.

The place has ghosts, she'd told him, but he was a man who tended to see what was before him so he'd dismissed her, telling her the dead don't haunt.

When Eugenie had hung up the telephone, she realized that she'd forgotten to tell Michael about Dean. Then from the window, she watched Dean go down to the fence and survey the posts, then kick them, one after another.

At least another month. Maybe two. That's what Michael had promised.

She pulled on her jeans, threw a sweater over her head, ran a brush through her hair. Getting the fence fixed would make her feel better, she reasoned as she went downstairs. As though by mending the fence, she too would be rendered stronger.

∾

Dean glanced out the window from Eugenie's bedroom. The sound of a car on the main road had put him on alert, but it drove on by. It was not Eugenie returning home. He continued checking the locks as he'd done in the other bedrooms.

Her bed was made, but there were clothes draped on it. A sweater had fallen to the floor and he bent to pick it up, then caught himself and left it. He went to her dresser, where he found a jar of ointment, her deodorant, hair elastics, a cup with the dregs of coffee. He ran his fingers along the chain of her necklace, then picked up a container, opened it and smelled the cream inside. He placed it back and glimpsed himself in the mirror, caught out by the image of the person he'd become.

23

He stroked his creased and bristly face, then pocketed a bar of handmade soap from a bowl.

On the landing, he found a framed photograph of Eugenie and a man he guessed was Michael. Picking it up, he dusted it with his sleeve and looked closely at the two of them, arms around each other as they stared straight into the camera, a snow-capped mountain in the background. Back down in the kitchen, he checked the windows and went out the back door leaving it unlocked, just as he'd found it.

The workshop was the only building Dean hadn't been in. He went there next. Its white walls, finished wood floor and track lighting gave the space an unexpected refinement. Eugenie had told him that they'd renovated the workshop when they first came to the place. Looking around, Dean realized it had barely been used. He sat on a stool and placed his hands on the table, examining the pegboard of tools on the wall before him. Hung in groups, there was a range of clamps, small saws, planes, some tools he didn't recognize. On the shelves were rows of nails, and several jars of metal bits and an array of wood pieces.

Dean opened a sketchbook and peered at the drawings, the notes, pictures of intricate designs pasted with labels. He went through the pages slowly, taking in the images of irregular-shaped furniture, chairs with three legs, a small cabinet with elongated legs that featured a hound chasing a fox etched into it, a coffee table with ocean waves crashing on a shoreline decorating its surface. Some pages had samples of geometric patterns, interlocking lines and angles to form a mosaic. Others were of specific images embedded into a design. A shell inside a box. A hand against the glass. He leaned in closer to study the image of the hand.

"What are you doing in here?" Without his noticing, Eugenie had stepped into the doorway.

Dean pulled himself up. "Don't you lock anything?" he said.

"What are you talking about?"

"Everything is open. The garage with all your tools. This workshop. You're asking to be robbed."

"I lock the house at night," she said, stepping aside as he walked out.

"Look, I'm sorry. I was looking for something."

Eugenie went inside the workshop then came back out, closing its door behind her. He looked over at the house he had just trespassed.

"I got the fencing," she said. "I left it in the car at the bottom of the lane. The posts will be delivered in the next hour."

They walked down to the fence in silence, Eugenie a half step behind, straining to keep up, and Dean striding briskly, trying to shake some force within, a wildness he feared he'd somehow revealed.

"Hold this." Dean handed her one end of the woven wire fencing and unspooled it along the fence line then went back to digging holes.

Soon she left him and went to the house to make coffee. By the time she returned, the truck was there with the posts. They unloaded the posts and placed each one near its hole. Dean took his spade and gestured for her to slide the first one in.

"My husband is a master carpenter," Eugenie said, gripping the post as Dean shovelled dirt around it. "He specializes in marquetry. That's where thin bits of wood are used to form geometric shapes or other decorative patterns that are inlaid on furniture to create a design."

"And he can only do this in Spain?"

"No." Eugenie answered quickly. "He did his apprenticeship there. The area he's in, near Granada, is known for its marquetry." She paused as Dean handed her the next post. "Now he has commitments."

"Commitments?"

"Projects. Things he has to finish."

"And you're here?" he asked.

"I inherited the place from my grandmother."

"Lucky you."

"Lucky me." She watched as he straightened the post, checking its alignment. "We moved here just over a year ago. Nearly 200 acres of land that includes woods that need clearing, fields that have gone to seed, a farmhouse that has not been occupied in nearly five years, a few outer buildings that, well, you can see how they're disintegrating, and a property that skirts a river that becomes marshland as it reaches the shore. Not exactly the best fresh start."

"Why did you take it on then?"

"It seemed like something we should do."

He frowned at her.

"I have plans to grow things, to plant an orchard, a garden of vegetables. I want a pantry full of things I've preserved. Maybe keep bees."

"Bees? Jesus …"

Eugenie went to her car and retrieved her water bottle. She drank then offered some to him. "You need to think of the future. You need to make plans. How else can you live?" she said, throwing the empty container on the ground.

It was late in the day when they finished, the dust a gritty veil on their hands and faces as they carried the tools back to the garage. They stood for a moment then Eugenie went inside and brought them each a beer. They drank in silence as they gazed in numb exhaustion at their day's work. Dean finished his quickly, then thanked her and left.

∽

Eugenie watched Dean walk away in the direction he'd come from that morning, not by the road but along a pathway that cut through the back of her property. She stood there for a few minutes, until he disappeared into the bush, then followed his path to the edge of the field to see where he'd gone. But she could no longer see any sign of him. The bushes and trees created a screen that allowed him to slip away, his exit obscured.

She went back to the house and locked the door behind her. She took out a plate of ham and threw together a salad, which she ate standing at the counter. After, she went to her bedroom, picked up the sweater that lay on the floor, shoved it in the drawer and stretched out on her bed. Having been outside for most of the day, the house now seemed strange to her, its quiet putting her on edge. She wished Michael would call but knew the time difference made that impossible. Instead she made a mental list of all she would tell him the next time they spoke.

The quiet of the night brought Eugenie back to those early days in Conchar and how the quiescence of the place was just what they'd needed. But even that had been disrupted by a neighbour's renovations. She and Michael had awoken one morning to the sound of machinery outside their window. It seemed impossible that someone could get a tractor down the path past the house, yet they managed to deliver more tiles, more plaster, more supplies.

Michael had peered through the window shutters, examining the light to see just how early it was. It was sometime past dawn, but there was no sign of the sun on the Sierra Nevada. They shuffled downstairs to the kitchen and Michael cowered at the back, away from the workers who were chatting outside the window in a way that indicated a mounting disagreement. They tried to ignore the voices, focusing instead on making coffee, getting the croissants from the cupboard, but then there was a knock at the front door. Michael opened the door to the man in charge of the construction project.

"Hola."

"No electricity," the man was pointing at his watch. "Por una hora," he said, swirling his finger around the watch face.

"No electricity until one o'clock? Or for one hour?"

"Si, si." The man was nodding as he stepped back from the door. Michael smiled the pale smile of a foreigner resigned to the strange patterns of an unfamiliar country and closed the door. Their home was plunged immediately into darkness. Weak slats of light came through the windows as they sat at the table with their café con leche and croissants. Eugenie knew that Michael was thinking of the work he had to do. She wanted him to go to Granada, or simply back to bed with her, because part of her wanted this to be just a holiday. But when the sun finally pierced through the shutters, it seemed a signal for him to get on with things.

Eugenie had followed Michael to his studio that day, ignoring his dismay at being disturbed.

"What are you working on?" she asked, wanting to find a

way into his private world, and he showed her the wardrobe that had been commissioned by a local from the expat community. He picked up the rod that looked like a sheaf of spaghetti, only it was of wood and metal, and held it out to her.

"This is where it starts with this particular technique," he said, running the tips of his fingers around the top. "You build the pattern putting together different strips … metal, a variety of woods, some people even use bone. Together it forms a design at the end."

Michael tipped it in her direction to reveal the geometric pattern, holding it like a baton, checking to see that the glue had held, his fingers working their way around, looking for flaws.

"I worked on this yesterday." He took it over to the saw and sliced off a medallion, letting it fall into his palm. "It's good," he confirmed, as he reached out to Eugenie to show her the result.

"It's beautiful," Eugenie said.

"I've a long way to go yet," he said, gesturing to the room in the back where the cabinet he'd built was stored. "I have to cut the rest and inlay them onto the cabinet. It's now just a large puzzle that I have to put together."

Then he reached over and kissed her, a sign that he was dismissing her.

Eugenie thought back to that time now, all alone in her grandmother's isolated homestead, which now seemed her very own project, one plucked from an opportune moment, one that would allow her to see through her own ambitions. Conchar seemed so far away, only a year ago in reality, but it was back when Michael was returning to someone they could both recognize after the devastating loss of his brother, and when talk of fresh starts had not yet included the farm.

Eugenie looked out her bedroom window and watched the starlings fly overhead. They swooped in and just as instantly spread out, finally gathering at the large oak tree behind the barn, their fluttery wings barely visible among the leaves. Then, startled, they were off again. She stood there until dusk watching their skittish movements.

∽

They were coming. Dean felt it in his body. Felt his heart lurch and pound, like a dog fighting a leash. He smelled the air burning, not smoke but rubber, the stench sickening. He crouched under a tree, the desert gone. He was in a jungle, shielded by the sunshade of lush green leaves overhead, fluttering against the light. He put his gun down, dropped to his knees. Then the sky exploded with the roar of helicopters. They hovered over him, their blades like a racing heart. He looked to Nick who was smiling peacefully, as if this were just a regular walk in the woods. He heard the screech of a rocket launcher, the clatter of a machine gun…

Dean woke up clutching his sleeping bag. The sound of his breath broke an otherwise silent dusk. There was no helicopter overhead.

The roar of a chainsaw had ripped through the forest to wake him from the nap he didn't know he was taking. He stepped out from his tent, the feeling of being under siege still with him, at odds with the familiar surroundings of pine and spruce. Somehow, the serenity made him feel worse. In his dazed state, still half dreaming, he looked around expecting to see Nick, but there was no sign of anyone, just the intermittent sound of the far-off chainsaw.

Dean stood up and wiped his face with his cold hands, wandered around the campsite, and finally slumped down on the end of a log. The forest was quickly darkening. He started a fire and held himself against its warmth as he watched new shadows slip in between the trees. He was thinking about Eugenie, wondering what she was doing, how she spent an evening like this one on her own. It would be good to stay here a while, but he figured she had a week's work for him at best. By then he'd have enough money to keep him going for a month or more if he kept living rough. How long he could keep going he had no idea, he didn't want to know. If he could scrape together enough food to live on, if he could keep warm and have a place to sleep, that was enough, wasn't it? He held his hands up to the fire, pressing his palms into the heat until he could no longer stand it. He did this over and over, as a game, as though this was a sensible way to occupy his mind.

The evening wore on with Dean becoming more restless until he remembered the button on his shirt that had come off. He fumbled through his gear looking for the tin that held the needle and thread and sat down, leaning into the light of the fire. He held the needle, his hand firm against his knee while he took aim with the thread. It was his older sister Victoria who'd taught him to sew, telling him a man ought to know how to work a needle as much as a saw. He missed his sister, now a nurse in Bangor, and wondered if he'd ever see her again. She would not be impressed with his half-hearted effort trying to get this button on. He muttered to himself as he jabbed at the hole, the thread bending, splitting. He began to lose patience, which he knew would get him nowhere. He tried several times, the thread quivering until at last, success. He guided it through the needle slowly then tied a knot, his fingers getting cold as the evening damp set in.

The fading sun scattered vivid patches of light on the forest floor, and Dean, looking up at the sudden illumination, distracted by its beauty, accidentally stabbed his finger. Blood dripped onto a leaf, then trickled off. It was getting too cold for sewing, but he needed to get the button onto his shirt before going to work in the morning. Beside him lay his hunting knife unsheathed, ready to slice the thread once the button was secure.

A flock of starlings few past, squawking and frenzied, just as he'd known them to be back home in Maine on summer evenings. Those nights sitting out on his deck drinking a beer, enjoying the peace of doing nothing, just sitting and listening. Not worrying about life and death, or a future, or where his next meal might come from. Not thinking about civilians or soldiers, nor any kind of duty to which he might feel obligated. And this memory, of the quiet and the birds, stung him so much that he put the shirt on, the needle still dangling, and shoved those thoughts of home out as if they never really belonged to him.

A rustle in the bush jolted him and he grabbed for his gun, his hand scrambling through the debris of clothes, food packets and utensils that lay around him, before he figured out that he no longer had one. Then came the swift realization that it was just a rabbit out in the woods, not an insurgent.

∾

"I want to build a chicken coop," Eugenie announced when Dean arrived the next day. She'd spent a restless night, awake for hours trying to prioritize plans that would keep Dean busy, and the chicken coop seemed a good place to start. "I was thinking of putting it beside the barn," she said, handing Dean a coffee. "That way we can see them, but they'll be away from Michael's workshop."

Dean went over to assess the area Eugenie had indicated. "I never thought of chickens as scenery, but it's your place."

She waited for him to offer his bit of advice. As she'd talked about her plans during the few odd jobs they'd done, Eugenie had discovered Dean had views on things that might be useful: companion planting and how to maximize the harvest, insect control and organic fertilizers. He'd offer advice in an offhand way. *Might be a good idea to set up some rain barrels over by the house. You should sketch your garden out in a notebook and plan the rotation for the next few years. You need to build a composter over by the barn.* This time he only grunted in agreement.

"Make a list of what we'll need and I'll run into town later," she said finally before heading into the house. She prepared some sandwiches, and when she brought them out, Dean came over to the bench and sat beside her. Over the past few days, they'd been working on a drainage trough outside the barn and she had started bringing Dean food because she noticed he only ever seemed to eat granola bars. She had started to talk about plans for the place as if he had equal say, and this was not lost on Dean.

"Where did you learn about farming?" she asked.

"I lived in the country growing up."

"So you know what it's like."

He looked at her.

"This hard life," she continued. "There is nothing easy in the country. Everything is tough, animals killing lesser animals, fields falling to seed. The isolation alone will kill you."

"And yet you're here."

"And yet I'm here."

"Why did you come back?"

She looked away from Dean. "We were at a standstill in England. Michael's brother had died. He discovered marquetry. It was the focus he needed. When I got this inheritance, it seemed an omen."

"So you bet your future on an omen."

"Something like that."

They worked until the day grew too warm. As the heat of the afternoon encroached, they sat at the kitchen table and made a list of supplies they would need for the chicken coop. They drank tea, and together they sketched a plan, talked about what kind and how many chickens. They ate sandwiches and she almost convinced him to go into town with her to get the material, but he told her he thought it best to stay and mark out the site. It was late afternoon by the time they got up from the table, having the sense that they'd accomplished a great deal, that they no longer needed to be wary, cautious in each other's presence, that they could get a few things done around the place if they worked hard, together.

By the time Eugenie got back from town he had set out stakes and strings so that she could envision the footprint of their design. As she emptied the supplies from the car she realized it had been more than a week since she'd spoken to Michael and she wondered what he'd think of the chickens.

"I'll get back at it tomorrow," Dean announced, packing up.

"Do you have far to go to your uncle's camp?"

"Not far. Just the other side of the hydro lines." He was gesturing over to the woods where he'd emerged these past days,

34

and she looked beyond in search of hydro poles. The bank of trees obscured any sign of them.

"Let me know if you need anything out there," she said after a moment, turning to the house.

From the kitchen window she watched him cross the yard and, ever involved in his work, he stopped to adjust two of the stakes, extending the line of the foundation for the chicken house. Eugenie admired his work ethic, or rather his allegiance to her dream of a better homestead. She continued to watch him as he measured, made notes in the notebook he carried, and marked the place where he would dig holes. Next time, she thought, she would pack him some food.

That night Eugenie dreamt of her garden. The rows were laid out as they were before Dean showed up and in her dream she was confused as to why it had changed. She was standing beside the garden watching the rain wash all the seeds into the river, so that it looked like the land was connected to the water with a network of muddy veins. There was nothing she could do but watch, feeling the loss of her garden as she witnessed it being flushed out to the river. Soon she became horrified as the vegetables started sprouting from the river, giant carrot tops poking through the surface, twirling bean plants spiralling sky-ward, enormous tomatoes hanging from tree-like plants.

She awoke in a panic, the image of the watery garden un-dulating in the river's current staying with her for some time until she was able to fall back into a calmer, more restful sleep.

The next morning was Saturday and, knowing Dean wouldn't be coming, she went to her garden. Unable to fully separate her dream from reality, she half-expected to see the flowering plants drifting in the river. But the garden was nothing like the one she had dreamt of. This one had appropriate-sized seedlings sprouting from the re-aligned rows.

Things had changed for her since Dean had arrived. She'd found her purpose in the place. The reasons for not coming back and taking on the farm had slipped away and it had begun to feel like a place she where she could feel settled, even while she waited for Michael.

She stayed in the garden until early afternoon, laying the groundwork for an arbour. She'd dragged down an old bench from the barn and spent the morning putting a frame around it, a place for the sweet peas and beans to climb, a place for her to sit and enjoy the space. Her thoughts strayed to Dean as she worked, wondering how he was spending his day off. He'd be pleased to see how the garden was coming along. They'd be eating their own food in a month or so, the food they'd grown themselves.

∽

Dean took the wire out and threw his pack on the ground. He measured a length, snipped it and began making a small loop, twisting the wire along one end. It was barely dawn, the coldest part of the day. He wished he had bothered to make coffee, but he had to get the snares in place early if he was to have any chance of catching a rabbit. He blew the chill from his hands and continued twisting the end of the wire, pulling at it to make sure it was secure. Then he threaded the other end through the loop to make the noose. He twirled the wire around with his thumb and forefinger, thinking about what a delicate killing machine it was.

The morning fog was lifting as he crawled along the forest floor to find a place to set the trap. He was looking for a narrow opening in the thick bush, a rabbit highway. He hadn't done this in a while, not since he was a teenager, and then it had been his father who usually found the best runs, a pathway surrounded by branches or rocks.

The sound of his breath helped him focus. He listened to the steady rhythm of exhale and inhale, which in the still, damp woods seemed amplified, as if inside a helmet. He held his concentration as he reached into an opening, a tunnel made of spruce boughs, and gently placed the wire trap. He draped the noose from a branch, leaving a four-inch gap from the ground as his father had taught him, and anchored it to another branch. Then he placed a few twigs to hold it in place and to camouflage the wire before turning back. He went to a nearby log where he half squatted, half sat, suddenly feeling that he was being watched. His breathing was heavier now and, in the dawn-lit forest, he did what he was trained to do, a quick assessment of any danger.

Sunlight shot through the scrawny trees. Dean jumped up, grabbed his pack and briskly moved on. He kept glancing back, the trees chasing him farther into the woods until he stumbled, his pack flying over his head as he rolled to the ground. He lay there for a moment, catching his breath, surveying as much as he could without moving his head, then jumped to his feet. A crackle in the bush and his body swivelled. Frantic, he looked around and saw a deer standing stock still, its eyes like fear itself. Both of them remained that way, frozen, until finally the deer cut through a path, his rump bobbing further into the bush. Dean set three more traps in the area then headed for the road that led to the highway.

This was his second day of getting up early to set snares for rabbits, but yesterday he'd had no luck. He had looked forward to skinning and then preparing the meat for a stew, using some of the dried food he had with him. But he hadn't caught anything. He'd lain in bed last night, going over the procedure his father had taught him as a boy, troubleshooting what had gone wrong with the day's traps. He'd woken determined to catch a rabbit today.

The new morning seemed full of good signs. His sleep hadn't been troubled by nightmares and, when looking for a place to set his snares, he'd found a patch of dandelion greens and wild garlic. He'd stuffed them into his bag, feeling his role as both hunter and gatherer complete.

It was a good two kilometres from here to the highway. Just up the road, where the truck driver had let him off the day he arrived in Canada, there was a gas station. He trudged through the damp woods, the smell of last winter's decay coming back to life in the spring warmth, that of wet animal pelts and musty aroma of rotting leaves filling his lungs like an astringent. He felt the air move through him, and wondered why this sensation should seem so foreign to him. He quickened his step to a slow jog, dodging branches, pushing away twigs that scraped past him.

He thought of those days in Maine, growing up near the woods, playing Cowboys and Indians, taking target practice, smoking dope, or just trying to get away from everyone. He'd built a fort once, dragging wood from his neighbour's shed, scraps they wouldn't notice gone, and for a long time he'd played there with the toy soldiers his father had given him until one day he felt that the game didn't make sense any more. He didn't know what to do with them, other than have them kill each other, and after a while that got boring. So he dug a hole and buried all his soldiers and moved on to video games.

He told that story a lot. In Fallujah, where he served eleven months in the infantry on his first tour of duty. Playing cards, getting drunk, telling stories. That's what they were good at. So he told his own story of how he got bored killing soldiers, and they'd all laughed because they were bored in their own way, waiting and not waiting for the war to get going. Working at jobs they could be doing in civilian life. Ignoring the constant edginess that hummed below the surfaces as they waited for their orders.

By the side of the road, Dean crouched under a spruce tree and watched people come and go at the gas station. He pulled out the book he'd been carrying since he left Iraq, one he'd taken from Nick when he was killed. *The Iliad*, it had been Nick's bible. He'd wave his tattered copy at Dean and tell him that the universal truth of war lay in the pages of the book. Dean had a hard time with universal truths. Especially now, with Nick gone.

Dean looked up to the thatch of branches that protected him from the rain and opened the book, read a few pages then put it away, the memory of Nick too strong. Thoughts of survival steadied him. He needed to keep warm, and he needed to eat.

Half an hour had passed, and Dean was no longer warm from the jog through the woods. He was shivering. He was dying for a coffee, or tea. Anything warm, and civilized. He could go back to camp and make one, but the effort seemed too much.

Instead he just sat there, staring and not really thinking about anything at all. He felt that he could stay there all day, watching the people pass by, watching their lives in this moment in time, wondering where they were headed, what they'd do when they got home.

Then a little boy ran across the parking lot at the same time a car pulled up to the pump, and Dean rose from his perch, about to call out. But something stopped him. His mind tripped into a distant memory. The boy in the parking lot gone, replaced with another boy, this one in Iraq.

The sharqi wind had whipped up the dust, so they hardly saw the boy who was kicking at some garbage. The soldiers kept watch on him. One, then another shouted, but the boy was lost in his own world. The sergeant started yelling to get that kid out of there. Rebels were coming. They were set to attack and the kid was still out there. The wind created a screen, and they lost sight of him completely. The sergeant shouted louder, the soldiers now agitated, and then a man appeared from nowhere. Dean hoisted his gun. Eyed him through the crosshairs. The long white gown, like a ghost that crept through the billowing dust, made him an easy target. Dean slid his finger onto the trigger just as the boy ran out of the cloud of dust. He dropped the gun and watched as the boy went to the man, who slapped him on the back of the head, scolding him as they walked back to the village.

Dean pulled out an apple from his pack, took a bite, then spit it out. It was starting to rot. Despite his hunger Dean couldn't stand to eat it. He flung it into the woods and stepped out of the bush. A car went past and he trotted a few feet along the road, noting how jittery he was. His plan was to go in, get a coffee and a sandwich, then walk around to the side of the building as if heading to the washrooms. From there, it was just a few steps back to the woods.

Dean walked into the store, feeling the rush of warm air and excessive lighting, and headed straight to the coffee bar. He tried not to look around but his survival training got the better of him and he did a quick survey of the room while he poured his coffee. In Iraq, a man talking on his cellphone might be an operative giving the clearance for bomb attacks. Dean had grown so used to being ready for anything that wartime vigilance had become his norm. He spilled his coffee over his fingers trying to get the lid on and reached for a napkin.

"You okay?" The woman next to him was pouring a coffee. He looked at her.

"Your hand okay?"

"Oh. Yes, it's fine." Dean shook his head. "I can never get these things on without spilling some."

At the cash, he grabbed a tin of travel sweets then took out a roll of bills, thankful that Eugenie had paid him in cash. He pulled out a twenty, and held it in front of him, waiting for the young man to ring in the few items he'd placed on the counter. The attendant was keeping an eye on the gas pumps outside, handing someone the keys to the washroom, reaching for Dean's money, all the while barely glancing his way.

The bell over the door rang as a new customer walked in. The cash register chimed. Two men talked loudly as they poured their coffees. Though the lights made him feel exposed, no one paid him any attention.

The attendant was holding his bag out to him, and by the time Dean grabbed it a glance of irritation overtook the young man's face. That will be the moment he remembers me, thought Dean. Up till then I was anonymous. People always remember the ones who are rude.

41

Dean edged around to the back of the store, then without checking whether he was being watched, he walked straight into the woods. Once there, past the bank of ferns and fallen branches, he slumped to the ground. He drank his coffee, his hand quivering, his heart racing, not sure if it was relief or contentment he was feeling.

When he was done, he trudged back to his camp, taking a detour to check on his snares. He'd killed three rabbits. He gathered them, laid them out on the ground before him, and one by one he jerked on the noose until the heads snapped off, tumbling onto a bed of pine needles. Then he stuffed the bodies into a bag and went back to camp.

∾

"I have something for you," Dean announced when they'd finished their work for the day. He handed Eugenie a package wrapped in a crinkled brown bag.

Eugenie pushed her hair back, then wiped her hands clean across the front of her shirt. She took it from him and sat down at the bench. "Travel sweets," she said, smiling, her fingers feeling the gold tin. She sat cupping the tin as if it were something precious, the clatter of tools disturbing the quiet as Dean packed up.

"I'm heading out," he said. He held her gaze for a moment then smiled as he reached for a cigarette.

"Okay. I'll see you in the morning then." She held up the tin. "Thank you."

He walked away, a trail of smoke lingering behind him.

She watched him as he walked along the pathway that led to the field at the back of the house. The moment he disappeared into the bush, she put the tin on the bench and hurried out after him, uncertain what she was doing, how far she would go. She felt at once foolish and excited, the adrenaline carrying her along the rugged path that Dean had tramped down. The abruptness of the adventure caused her to shiver. She tugged at her sweater, ducking every few minutes as if anticipating that Dean would turn around and catch her. But he kept on going, never once looking back.

By the time they passed the tree line, she was beyond explanation if discovered so she stayed low, occasionally peering over bushes that skirted the entrance to the woods. At one point she lost sight of him as he disappeared into the trees, and she scuttled forward until she caught up with him again. The woods were denser than she'd expected, and soon she had the feeling she'd gone too far. The glare of the sun deceived her, bringing unexpected shadows and an abrupt dimming as she slipped below the thick cover of spruce boughs. A breeze stirred the trees, their sudden soughs like a deep moan pushing her along.

She had no idea how far in she was and soon a flutter of claustrophobia came upon her as she lost sight of him again, panic urging her forward as she moved with an unsteady trot. It was all she could hear, the swish of her pant legs, the crunch of each step on pine needles. The sudden heavy creaking of two trees, their trunks leaning into the other, swaying as if in some drunken arboreal dance, stopped her. The sound, primal, a reminder of all the haunted woods in fairy tales she'd read as a child, convincing her to go back.

Looking around, she became disoriented, unsure of which way she'd come. She was in a thicket of bushes, no trail to rely on, no instincts to point her in the one true direction she needed.

Eugenie thought of the map they'd been given with the deed. Mentally tracing her steps, placing the house, the spruce forest, the wood lot, the pond, she tried recreating all the elements of the crude map. She tried to remember the size of the forest, how far in she might be.

She didn't hear Dean until he spoke.

"You lost?" he asked.

"Oh my God," she said when she saw him standing next to a tree some ten feet away. "Oh my God," she repeated, this time feeling less startled and more concerned with being discovered. "You scared me."

"Where are you going?"

"For a walk," she answered.

"Well, let's go."

"What?"

"Let's go. I'll show you what you want to see." He went on ahead a few feet before turning to make sure she was following him.

"What are you talking about?"

He didn't answer. He just kept walking through the bush.

"It's not far." He was up the hill and she knew that soon he would be out of sight again. She started walking toward him, stumbling over moss covered trunks, batting twigs out of the way, quietly panicking that he might leave her behind, lost with no way out.

She nearly ran into him when she got to the top. He stepped back, motioning to a spot in the distance. She looked over and saw nothing. For the first time she had a feeling she might be in danger.

"There it is," he said.

44

"There what is? Oh." Her eyes lighted on a small tent hidden in the undergrowth.

"My home. It's what you were looking for, right? Where I come from."

She stepped back, her eyes looking for an escape. She felt her face go hot as she shifted from one foot to the next, back and forth as if she were getting ready at the blocks, shaking loose her hands, moving to distract him from the anxiety he must surely notice. "What's this about?"

"You don't need to be afraid," he said firmly.

"I'm not afraid." She tried to laugh but really only sniffed.

"It's temporary."

"What does that mean?"

He reached out, as if to guide her, but she was too skittish now. He dropped his arm and settled back away from her.

"I ran away from the army," he said finally. "The US Army."

"Oh."

"I just need some time to figure things out."

Eugenie stopped rocking and turned to the direction she'd come from.

"Why are you here?"

"I know the woods along the Maine border. I found an isolated spot, crossed over and a trucker picked me up on this side. I got out on the highway near here."

"How long have you been living here?"

"Nearly four weeks."

"I don't understand."

"I'm a deserter." He looked at her, then, as if giving up his hold on her, walked away. "I need to figure out what to do."

"What to do?"

She looked down at the camp and saw his clothes folded neatly on a log, his pots and utensils spread out by the stove, the tent, green and low, in line with the bushes nearby. She walked slowly down the hill. "I think I ought to go back now," she said.

"Okay," he said, stepping away as if to make room for her departure.

"I have to go," she repeated.

"I can make you tea."

Eugenie laughed at this, a nervous chortle, then caught herself and said, "No thanks, another time."

They stayed a few minutes longer, the stillness disorienting. Instead of leaving, she sat down as if needing to rest.

"I was supposed to report for duty a month ago," Dean said at last. "I did my tour, but they're calling me back." He turned away so she barely heard him. "I've had enough."

"I see," said Eugenie.

"Are you going to turn me in?"

"It's not my business," she said, suddenly tired.

"No one knows I'm here."

"I know."

"I meant the authorities."

"And so you'd like a blind eye?"

"Something like that."

The forest darkened by the sudden setting of the sun, and Eugenie jumped to her feet. "I need to get back."

"Of course," he said. Seeing the look of concern on her face, he added, "I'll take you as far as you want to go."

"Just to the edge of the forest," she murmured as she walked off.

Where the forest ended, the open field was a relief. Eugenie started to speak and then stopped, holding her hand out vaguely towards him.

"Do you need anything?" she said, looking toward the house.

"No."

They remained rooted, trying to find a way to leave, when a pack of coyotes crept out of the woods, pausing to look at the two of them. For a fleeting moment, they were trapped. The six animals, tawny furred, straggly and dismissive, continued walking in a semi-circle past them, looking over their shoulders as if to ensure they would not be followed back into the woods.

Dean watched as they headed in the direction of his camp, then turned to Eugenie.

"I'd better get back there."

"You want to be their dinner?"

"They're more interested in my food." He took a few steps away from Eugenie then turned back to her. "Am I going to be okay here tonight?"

Eugenie looked at him, thinking of the coyotes, wondering herself whether he might be under threat. Then their conversation sprang back to the forefront, alongside the revelation that he'd been living in the wild all this time, and how the long hours working for her must've almost been a reprieve for him. He had an untold history, one that was altogether different than she'd imagined, and on an impulse that could make sense of none of this, she leaned in and kissed him on the cheek. "Yes, of course," she whispered, then turned and walked home.

༄

Dean stood by the stream looking at his hands. He wasn't sure what he was supposed to be doing. He didn't know how long he'd been standing there, but he knew he was awake and standing in broad daylight, his soap and toothbrush nearby, the morning sun leaving spidery shadows on the forest floor. The shrill call of a bird was followed by a wave of leaves rustling overhead.

He hadn't slept much since last parting ways with Eugenie. Fear and excitement, at being caught, at being wanted, had kept him awake until nearly dawn. He hadn't been close to a woman, or anyone, since before his tour of duty. After war, having people close to him felt like a responsibility he was no longer prepared to take on. But that kiss. He hadn't seen it coming, and now he couldn't make it go away.

He bent down and splashed his face, wiping his hands over his hair again and again until he was soaked. He quickly brushed his teeth, threw his soap and toothbrush into his bag and went back into his tent. He knew he was expected at the homestead, but what if Eugenie had woken full of regrets, what if she finally realized who he was and what that could mean for her? A moment of apprehension stalled him. The thought that Eugenie could contact the authorities and be done with him if she came to her senses, had a change of heart, left him paralyzed in the stifling tent. But he wanted to see her, curious how she would be towards him, so he pulled on his boots, slid out of the tent and went to work.

When he got to the homestead, Eugenie was gone. Her car wasn't in the yard. The house was locked up. He walked around the lot, then over to the hill that overlooked the garden, but there was no sign of her. He shouted her name, but there was no response.

Dean hurried from one building to the next, fearing the worst: she had gone to the authorities. Bolting back to his camp like a startled deer, he hopped over bushes and swung wildly at branches as he went. He couldn't survive in jail or the army, not after everything he'd gone through, there was no going back. Once inside his tent, his body steamed from exertion, the hot air felt like he was breathing inside a plastic bag. With nowhere else to go, he pulled the sleeping bag around him and closed his eyes.

This is where Eugenie found him two hours later. "Dean?" she asked, holding back the tent flap. "Are you okay?"

"What?" Dean pulled himself up on one elbow and wiped his face with his other hand. The tent felt stuffy, airless. He had to get out in the open.

"I've brought you some food."

"Food?" On the log by the fire pit he saw a basket. Inside he found some chicken, bread, an apple, and water.

"Thank you. I'm sorry." He took a drink of water. "I was worried … the police. I don't want to go to jail."

Eugenie put her hand on his shoulder. "You thought I'd turned you in?"

"Let's just say I didn't know what to think."

"Please, sit down. Eat. It'll make you feel better. There's no need to worry."

Dean ate the bread and chicken while Eugenie grabbed a pot, filled it with water and set it on the propane burner.

"I'll make some tea." She smiled encouragingly. "Next time I'll bring you something stronger to drink."

"I wouldn't say no to that."

The water boiled, and when the tea was made she sat next to him.

"I can help you if you like."

"I don't know what I need right now. I didn't sleep last night."

"At all?"

"Not much. I was worried that I'd spooked you. I was worried that you'd turn me in."

In that moment, Eugenie clutched Dean's arms and leaned in to kiss him. Dean felt her lips press into his, felt the tug of her hands as she held onto his arms, the confusion of the moment overriding any sense of pleasure he might feel. Then he did feel. His bristled chin meeting her face, his hand brushing back strands of her hair. Dean pulled her into him, slid his hand under her shirt and felt the warmth of her back.

Later, she roamed the campsite in his shirt, her bare legs shivering in the breeze. He could tell by the way she got dressed that she felt guilt, perhaps even regret. Things were happening at a pace that startled both of them. She said she had to get home and refused to let him walk back with her. She had a frantic, searching look in her eyes, he could see that she was trying to get back to Michael, to herself as someone who didn't sleep with strangers in the woods.

∾

The days grew longer, and the warm air announced that summer was not long in coming. The garden Eugenie had planted at the beginning of the season was starting to bulge with vegetables, as if tempting the dream she'd had to come true. The next time she spoke to Michael she told him about her dream. "My garden spilled into the river," she said, trying to sense his interest through his silence. "There were plants sprouting in the water, giant plants."

50

"Giant plants," Michael said on the other end. "What are you talking about?"

"Never mind. Nothing." Eugenie sat down at the table and closed her eyes. "How's your wardrobe coming along?"

A hesitation, another second of silence that told her that again she was not at the top of his mind.

"Fine. I'm down to the details now."

"Where the devil lives," Eugenie muttered.

"What's that? I didn't hear you."

"Nothing. Listen I've got to tell you about Dean."

"Yes, I got your message. I can't believe how much he's got done. He's a real find for us. I was thinking we should keep him on for the summer if he's willing, just in case."

"Just in case of what?"

Another hesitation. Eugenie tried to imagine what Michael wanted to tell her.

"I'm meeting the customer tomorrow in Lanjarón. I hope there won't be any changes."

"Michael, what are you talking about?"

"I've had to change the design. It wasn't working so I made some alterations. I need to get it approved. I'll know tomorrow."

"And what does that mean?"

"It could be a delay in coming home."

This time the silence was hers. Michael was waiting for her reaction. "We can't keep doing this," she said finally.

"Eugenie…" he tried to reason with her.

"How long this time…"

They hung up. She was losing track of who Michael had become, someone who no longer listened, who seemed barely there when they spoke. She had called him in search of a rea-

51

son to stop her feelings for Dean before things went any further. It would have been so easy for Michael to call her back to reason after all they'd been through, memories that even now she clung to. Lanjarón, she thought, remembering the last time they had gone there together. That was where it all began to unravel for them, their relationship as precarious as the twists and turns of the impossible mountain road, a ledge etched into rock, the only road to the town.

Spain was meant to be temporary, a bolthole while Michael completed his apprenticeship. They had just learned that Eugenie had inherited her grandmother's house in New Brunswick, and for her at least, it had given their lives new urgency. Now with the house, they could move on to something permanent.

But Michael had to meet Antonio in Lanjarón, the village of ham and water. They'd been there the year previous for the festival, a ritual celebration of the two things for which the town was known. She and Michael had watched the locals hanging off balconies, emptying buckets of water over crowds. Colourful lights draped along the main road, and even the crumbling castle stuck out on the rocky promontory underwent a festive facelift as a backdrop to the fireworks, the parade, and the party that would go on until dawn. All to celebrate water. And ham. But this year they would not see any of it. Eugenie hoped they would be in Canada by then.

They were on their way to see Antonio, the master craftsman with whom Michael apprenticed, to discuss future projects, their move to Canada, what remained of the apprenticeship. She could have left him to go on his own, let him discuss his plans with Antonio without her interference, but Michael seemed so low that morning she felt that she ought to go with him. She'd brought his coffee to him in bed, where he seemed to linger as if ill. He would not reveal what was on his mind, saying that he was merely tired. And she'd left it at that. After breakfast, she told him she would go to Lanjaron with him.

They could see the white-washed buildings of Lanjarón as they weaved around the valley. Like boxes stacked haphazardly, the village was built according to the landscape of the Alpujarras Mountains.

The area was once filled with Spanish Muslims, the Moors who fled to the hills rather than convert to Catholicism when King Ferdinand and Queen Isabella came to power. Lanjarón was thought to be inaccessible to King Ferdinand's men. But Ferdinand led his troops through a roundabout route on the steep mountainside to a point overlooking the town. The towns-people put up a brave fight, but many were killed and those who survived became slaves. It seemed such an insignificant town to have such a bloody, deceitful history. That should have been her first warning, Eugenie thought later.

Antonio was waiting for them at a café. He greeted them a bit gruffly, his English like a sour taste he needed to rinse away. He asked them if they'd like a drink. Eugenie declined, deciding she'd leave them to talk. Antonio summoned a measure of graciousness and directed her to the pathway that led to the Moorish castle nearby. But Eugenie stopped at a café just up the street instead. Through its window she could see the two men talking, Michael showing his designs, Antonio's enthusiasm evident. Eugenie felt some relief to see Michael happy. He had become immersed in his work, so much so that she wondered if it might be too much. But seeing him like this convinced her that his venture into marquetry had been what he needed to recover from

53

his brother's death. After so many months this had opened up something in him.

Eventually she went to the Moorish castle as directed, but the heat and the fact that the crumbling ruin held little fascination for her sent her back to the main street and to the café to join Michael. He smiled when she approached him, a social smile she rarely saw in private, and as he stood to pull out a chair for her, again not something he normally did, she wondered what influence Antonio might have over him.

"I was just telling him about Canada," Michael said as she sat down.

"The country or our plans?"

Michael threw her a mildly scolding look and Eugenie ordered a glass of beer from the passing waiter. "I told him about our plans to move there. To set up my workshop. To settle in your grandmother's house."

Eugenie looked at Antonio, taken aback by his look, which told her he did not approve.

"Antonio has a few projects he'd like me to take on," Michael said. "Before I leave."

"Before you leave?"

"They're good commissions." Michael's voice was low and she felt a hint of pleading in it.

"Will you take them?" she asked, now facing him as though Antonio were no longer there.

"Yes, I thought I would."

She looked at the two men who seemed to be avoiding any eye contact with her. A conspiracy that left her out.

"You must do the commissions then."

A half hour later they said their goodbyes and headed for

the car. Eugenie felt that perhaps Michael might fill her in on his meeting, tell her more about the commissions, but he had gone quiet again.

"Lanjarón has one of the greatest rates of longevity in the world," Michael said finally as they drove out of the village. "It's the spa baths with their medicinal mineral waters that do it."

"Are you suggesting we should move here instead?" Eugenie said, her tone crisp. But Michael only gave her a quick glance and then focussed back to the road, as if he was already in Spain by himself and she was back in Canada.

Summer

THEY SPENT MORNINGS AT THE HOUSE. Dean would come to her just after dawn, kiss the sleep from her eyes then move in beside her, the heat of her body radiating through him. Eugenie would surface from a deep sleep and nestle in, reaching her arms around him, eyes barely open.

June's heat had pushed the crop along, then July brought indiscriminate rains. After a solid week of it, they were left with a mess of runaway weeds and leggy plants. The wind had changed, the air turned warm again, the dampness evaporated, and they were left to enjoy the languorous July days. In the garden, they worked on their hands and knees pulling weeds, harvesting the first crop of arugula and lettuce.

It wasn't like this every day, but increasingly so. They had settled into rituals that marked them as a couple, a domestic idyll that Eugenie had always wanted of this place but could have never imagined taking root in these conditions. The pathway of trampled ground had established a permanency to his camp so that she had no problem finding him if she followed it. On mornings that he stayed behind in his forest camp, Dean ate a cold breakfast of granola, lit a small fire to heat water for shaving and for tea. A nylon rope along one side of the camp held his drying clothes, and at night he strung up any food items to store in a cotton bag.

Eugenie settled into the affair, and tried to partition her feelings so that thoughts of Michael only surfaced when he called.

Most of all, she liked that Dean listened, so basic a skill that Michael seemed to have lost in the past few years. And so she found herself speaking freely as they worked, telling Dean the history of the place, her life there. Despite the secrecy the affair demanded, his presence that spring and into the summer had, if nothing else, revealed to her that she was becoming more open herself, that she was no longer self-conscious about her past.

"My grandmother killed a man here. It was her cousin, so of course that made it worse. He was in her blind spot." Eugenie shoved a handful of weeds in the basket at the end of the row. They'd gotten a late start in the garden and now with the sun directly above they could only manage three of the eight rows. The heat forced them to take a break, and she told him the story of her grandmother. "She didn't see him behind her truck. He used to come over all the time, drink tea, talk politics. She just didn't know he was there. Sometimes I think this place is possessed."

"What happened to her?" Dean stood, stretched his back and looked around. "After the accident, I mean."

"Nothing. They investigated but there were no charges. She was an odd woman. Paranoid. My grandmother had bit of a reputation; she had a problem with authority. The accident happened not long after we came to live with her. My parents died in a car crash so the tragedies all kind of blended together."

"This place has some kind of past." He stood, clutching bunches of kale, dumping them in the nearby basket. "Speaking of which, there's something I want to show you."

"What is it?"

"Come with me."

There was no path where they entered the woods, but the bush soon became sparse. He walked in the direction of his camp then veered off, leading her through a prickly thicket. Eugenie picked her way through the sharp, brittle weeds, glancing back toward the house.

They tramped through the understory of the forest, knee-high in foliage for twenty minutes, and when they reached an opening, Dean stopped and pointed to a shack nesting in a cluster of blueberry bushes. "It's a sauna," he said. "Or at least it used to be."

"A sauna?"

"There's a wood stove inside, a bit rusty but still…" He was walking down the hill now with Eugenie close behind.

"My grandmother had a sauna?"

The shack, made of cedar boards, stood darkened by the shade of two spruce trees. There was a window at each end, a crack in one, and on the door a lock dangled open, its innards rusting. They walked to the threshold where leaves and pine needles lay gathered in mouldering clumps. Nearby, a stream trickled beneath a shroud of low-lying bushes. Eugenie touched the outside wall, as if trying to place the building in her memory.

"What was she doing with a sauna?" she asked again. Those days of roaming the fields with Ivy, or by herself; it seemed impossible that they never found this building. She felt a sense of loss in this discovery, as if she'd misplaced a crucial childhood memory.

"If I could move my camp here, maybe sleep inside, or just leave my gear here…" Dean looked at Eugenie. "What do you think?"

Eugenie brushed the spider silk from her fingers, her eyes still focussed on the building. "Maybe we should wait," she said, turning to him.

"Wait? For what?"

"I don't know. It's just … it's too much to take in."

"Okay. No problem. Waiting is my specialty." Dean went to the threshold. "It's one of the best training exercises the army gives you." He stepped inside and scraped away the pine needles in the doorway with his foot, then turned to look at her. He stood rigid, as if at attention, as if forcing some other version of himself on her. "In the army we waited for orders, for a plan, for the enemy to make a move. Then we'd go out on patrol and wait for the next blast, for that bump in the road to finally blow up the Humvee, for the bullet that finds its way around the Kevlar helmet." He paused. "So sitting here in the woods, doing some work for you, waiting to see if I can move into a sauna, is not going to be a problem."

"Stop. I didn't choose for this to happen. For you to move here. To be alone here to make decisions."

"Do you think this is what I want?" He swept his arm around the camp. "I'm asking you to help me choose between bad choices. I can't very well move into the house with you."

Eugenie suddenly saw how hard it must have been for Dean to ask her to move to the decaying sauna, his dignity diminished already. She went to the window, looked out at the stream, thinking of him alone here in the dark, hooded by trees, the night dew bringing on a chill, the nocturnal animals out on patrol. Up to now it had been like an extended camping trip, when he walked back into these woods she could stop thinking about how he lived, go back to her other life.

She walked around the building, and saw that it appeared structurally sound after all these years of neglect. She was thinking she could bring him furniture, a blanket, a lantern, a bottle of whiskey. In her mind, the camp was well placed, imperma-nent, out of the way, but it could be a place where Dean would feel more settled; there was no way she could deny him a roof over his head, however modest. They could each have a home here, she thought, the space they needed.

Home and space, she'd had to redefine both lately. These days when Dean left her to go back to his camp, Eugenie retreated to her room, to a bed weighed down under a pile of quilts, a return to herself. It was hard to know what to expect in this place that she'd anticipated as a future but was still mired in a past. And now there was this unplanned present to contend with. Eug-enie's memories of the homestead as a child were so scattered they seemed to leap across years at a time. In the time before their parents died when she used to come visit her grandmother, her sister Ivy rarely came with her. One child was all her grand-mother could handle. For years Eugenie was puzzled about why she was sent off to see her acerbic grandmother at all. Then later, she and her sister arrived when there was no one else to care for them, orphaned as teenagers, and spent years listening to their grandmother railing against the Communists, the Vietnam War, the Russians, as if she had something personal at stake.

There had always been a sense of exile to this place that she could never understand. And now, years later, among the black-flies and mosquitoes of summer, it was still serving as an exile to all those who claimed it. She was alone and not alone. It seemed the fate of living here. This time it was her property. And Mi-chael's. Michael should be here but he wasn't. Dean shouldn't be here but he was. And now Dean was taking root in the place.

"It seems in good shape," she said as she wrapped her arms around him by way of acceptance and apology. "No one would know, I suppose. If you hadn't shown me, I wouldn't even have known it was here. I'm sorry for stalling. You were right to be upset. We need to be open with each other. We need to be gentle with each other. Things are complicated enough."

∽

There were things Dean had trouble remembering. He'd begun to write things down. He had started a ritual each morning, making his coffee, eating his breakfast, his notebook and pen out on a log waiting for another piece to come through. Some mornings he added five or six things. Some days he remembered nothing. He sat leaning against a tree, pen in hand, working away at his memories.

He had started whittling a slingshot, something to occupy his hands while he tried to trace his memories. This became part of his ritual. Sitting, thinking, whittling, and sometimes jotting down something he recalled. Next to him, his dishes, pots, propane stove all lined up on a board he'd dragged from the farm. The sauna was still empty, the door closed. He had yet to move in. Instead he'd set up camp outside and, feeling more stable since he'd returned from Iraq, he tried to recall the things he had forgotten.

He wondered what the optimum level of remembering should be. He needed to remember enough to feel that nothing was hidden, but he also didn't want to start digging up memories he couldn't handle. Trying to get the right combination was important. There were times Dean wished he could talk to his father. He'd sit there mornings, daydreaming about the conversations they'd have, Dean telling his father the things he'd seen, the lunacy of bad commanders, the tough loss of a friend. He'd talk to his father about the men and how some of them got on his nerves because they were so stupid or loud or smartass or poor. And then there were those who he'd called better friends than any he had ever known. When he imagined these conversations, he inevitably realized that his was just another fucking lousy war, just like Vietnam had been a fucking lousy war, but neither he nor his father would ever say such a thing to the other.

Now he was just trying to remember, like the name of the soldier he'd sat next to on the way home. They talked for several hours on the plane, and if time had allowed they might have become friends. But now Dean couldn't think of his name, and it bothered him.

Once, one of the soldiers had a birthday and they'd celebrated by tying him up and painting a moustache on him with black shoe polish. Dean couldn't remember the rest of the evening, just the soldier shouting obscenities when he got free, smearing the polish across his face with the back of his arm before going back to drinking his beer. There were other things: the red-faced cook who served up the food in the mess hall; the sour smell of ammonia from the soldiers who'd become dehydrated; the moisture-seeking flies who crawled into his mouth when he was talking. All pieces of the story.

Dean remembered the day they went out to escort some new recruits. Going along the sandy road looking at the grey sky in the distance. Carter, driving the Humvee, complained about the storm that would turn the dusty hellhole into a muddy hellhole. Then a kaleidoscope of metal. The Humvee in front of them had been hit. Dean remembered it lifting in the air like it was a toy projectile, flying skyward as if a mirage.

That was all there was. His memory slammed shut like a prison door. He was left with his imagination. The fiery landing, the rush to rescue the men inside, a soldier screaming so much it seemed a different layer of hell, someone else's story. Carter had told him the rest. Carter, who wanted to talk about it and Dean who listened because he had no choice. Dean couldn't add anything to Carter's account because his version of the memory was forever stuck in the Humvee as it exploded.

That memory wasn't his to own, but the guilt was something altogether different. Guilt was a stain he couldn't get rid of. They had taken their eyes off the ball that day. They hadn't seen the IEDs. A thin wire across the road, a stray can, a pile of rubbish; you had to suspect everyone, inspect anything.

Guilt sticks to you; they told him that early on. Don't feel guilty about the fact that you're still alive and your buddy isn't. Don't feel guilty that the soldier next to you in the Humvee now has no legs. Don't feel guilty about the poverty and poor living conditions the Iraqis suffer. Dean got tired of feeling guilty and tired of the army telling him how he ought to feel.

The manual told soldiers they needed some stress but not too much. Stress has many positive benefits. Stress provides us with challenges; it gives us chances to learn about our values and strengths. Dean wondered what the optimum level of stress should be. He figured it would be damn hard to get to it. How many times did he have to be shot at, how many times did he need to see a body part where it shouldn't be, see blood on his hands? Even after a year he didn't know if he'd reached his optimum level because it felt like it never got any better.

And now he sat in the woods, all alone, no threat of IEDs, trying to recall each incident, bit by bit. He was mentally preparing to turn an abandoned sauna into a sanctuary. There was a woman nearby who perhaps loved him, or was at least conflicted about him, though he knew for certain how he felt. By god, he was almost happy. He had seen enough of life's darker underbelly to not bother with such trivial conflicts: you either loved someone or you didn't. The feeling lived in your gut.

It felt like such a luxury to rebuild his memories from this safe distance, the only worry that he might not be telling the truth, the complete and absolute truth. But he feared that, by looking too intensely, he would force his memories away, the focus obliterating events as if they never happened. It seemed that there was a good deal that could be omitted from the story if only he decided it didn't have to be recalled, and this troubled Dean.

∾

They'd spent the morning in the garden harvesting the carrots, bushels layered with straw, then a layer of carrots forked from the earth, then straw, then carrots. They did the same with beets, then they picked beans and some lettuce. They'd arranged for their neighbour to harvest the hay in a few weeks and they were talking about doing some canning. But for now, back in the forest, they could rest. They were outside the sauna, sitting back on a cushion of moss. Closing her eyes, Eugenie reached for Dean, her fingers lighting on his chest, his beard, his brow.

A few drops of rain splattered around them. Soon trickles began to make their way through the spruce branches.

"Come on." Dean took her hand and they went inside. The rain came down harder. Dean's hand smoothed the droplets on her cheek as he bent down to kiss her. The damp wind sifted through the sauna walls, and they held on to each other for warmth. She closed her eyes and listened to the forest sounds, the trees creaking, the flutter of leaves and the silence in between, the forest as much a refuge to her as it was to Dean.

"You'll need to insulate this place before fall."

"Are you saying I can stay?"

"I got a call from Michael last night. He doesn't know when he'll be back."

"I'm sorry to hear it."

"So you'll want to keep warm while you're here."

"I've got a plan worked out. I'll need some of your hay."

"Take what you need." Eugenie leaned into him, her head resting on his shoulder. "Tell me how you ended up here," she murmured. "I think I need to hear you talk right now."

"My father was in the army too, in Vietnam. He sometimes talked about draft dodgers or deserters coming to Canada. They'd cross over into Quebec and New Brunswick and live in the backwoods. He'd heard about a place where the locals used to protect them. The RCMP would go looking for them and the people in the community would hang a Hudson's Bay blanket out on the clothesline as a signal for them to stay in hiding. Once the blankets came down the men knew they were safe to come out of the woods."

Eugenie felt the stillness of his body, so calm it seemed he was barely breathing. She pressed her hand against his chest as if to feel for a heartbeat. There had been other moments like this, she'd noticed. Moments when he was reduced to something inhuman, like he'd lost himself somehow or part of him had drained away. She'd been talking around the subject of war for weeks, looking for a way in, not wanting to upset him. Moving

68

into the sauna had seemed to settle him. She'd seen something shift in him, a readiness to talk about things without his armour being raised.

"You've never talked about why you left."

"I signed up to get an education, not to go to war. I did eleven months, then our tour was extended another eight months. When I came home I knew I could never go back there. There are not a lot of options when you make that decision."

The rain stopped as suddenly as it started. When they went outside, the woods had deepened in tone, the green of the leaves vivid, the tree trunks wet black. They talked about mulching the garden, the pruning of the apple trees, the winter repairs. Eugenie suggested they have dinner together at the house, to celebrate the work they'd done. Dean, without hesitating, agreed. It felt like they could live in this bubble they'd cultivated indefinitely.

∾

Dean emerged from the bush, his clothes fresh from the clothesline, their wrinkles slowly flattening against his body. He was freshly shaven, and his hair, which normally looked like he'd just taken his hat off, was slicked back still drying from a frigid washing.

He saw Eugenie step out onto the porch and spot him in the field. His steps quickened as she came to him, moved by the effort she made, the will to be near him. When they came together by the new fence, *their* new fence, he hesitated, wanting to say something meaningful, an expression of the joy he felt in being with her, but he was too overwhelmed, able only

69

to tell her she looked good. She led him back to the house and brought out a beer for each of them.

"I quit, you know," he said, lighting a cigarette now. "Before I went to Iraq, I hadn't smoked for over five years. Some soldiers thought going to Iraq would be a good time to kick the habit. Cold turkey. Our commanding officer told them they might want to reconsider. The CO knew they couldn't quit. They'd just end up bumming off other soldiers. Five years without a cigarette, then three months in Iraq and I was back in the game."

They were quiet for a moment, looking out across the fields, awkward in the formality of the occasion. He glanced her way a few times, expecting her to guide them through the evening. Then he stood up and went to the doorframe testing the wood to see if it had rotted.

"It's good to hear you talk about it," said Eugenie. "The war I mean."

"Everyone has their own version," Dean said, accepting the dishes she handed him to set the table. "The war you see on television, the war I saw on the ground, the war politicians think they see, the war the military brass want to see. I've seen newscasts with Humvees roaring across the desert, sand flying from the tires with men carrying flags as if it's just part of a patriotic movie. No one bothers reporting about the stinking heat, the air that smells like a sewer. No one mentions sitting in a Humvee crawling at twenty miles an hour waiting to be blown up, or a trigger-happy sergeant who thinks he sees a gun under every man's robe."

"We didn't see the war coming." Eugenie said. "We just didn't think it would happen. We were so wrapped up in our own world, and this seemed so much bigger than us, we just couldn't take it on."

Eugenie went inside and Dean followed. She opened the oven, poked around at the chicken inside, then closed the door, her face flushed.

"You okay?" he asked, as she touched her forehead and sat down again.

"Michael's brother died just before the war," Eugenie said. "We were in a bit of a daze."

He set down his beer and massaged her shoulders. She kissed his hand as it passed across her collarbone. The breeze lifted the curtain behind her, and somewhere in the distance they heard a truck horn rip through the stillness. She turned the stove off, took his hand and led him upstairs. Their lovemaking was frantic, hurried, as if Michael weren't four thousand miles away.

Later, when they came back downstairs, Dean carved the chicken while she made a salad. He rushed ahead and devoured his food, then stopped himself when he noticed how she lingered over hers, her fork and knife placed casually on her plate as she drank from her glass of wine.

"I've been living like an animal. It shows," Dean said. "Living out there, at times there is a quiet that feels like you're the only one in the world. Other times, it can feel like the centre of some universe you're not part of. I heard some animals outside the other night. They weren't into my food; they just seemed to be walking around the campsite. It was strange. It felt like I was back in Iraq. They could smell me, they just couldn't see me. I was the outsider, the trespasser."

"I can't imagine what it would be like," Eugenie said, setting her hand on his. "To be an enemy, to be shot at."

"Once, when we were under fire, I ran down the stairwell and found one of our soldiers on the floor, gripping the wall, too frightened to shoot at the muzzle flashes out the window. It doesn't happen often, but it happens." Dean wanted to explain the soldier's mind to her in that moment when they take aim, the technical calculations—shot geometry, yardage, wind, and how some soldiers run scared. But these were details meant for soldiers.

They didn't hear the gravel crunching in the lane until the car was nearly upon them. Dean half rose in his chair, then sat back down. Eugenie went to the door. Out the window, Dean saw the car pull up near the porch, and the man driving step out.

"Hello," he called. "I got your message."

"Message?"

"Jack Butler. You left a message a while back. You wanted me to inspect your barn."

"My barn?" Eugenie looked at Dean in confusion. Finally she said, "Wasn't that a few months ago?"

"I've been out west. I just got back a few days ago. I can have a quick look now," Jack said.

"I've hired Dean since contacting you," she said as Dean stepped out onto the porch. "He's been doing some repairs around here."

"It seems pretty solid to me." Dean said.

They walked to the barn and Eugenie and Dean held back so that they could observe Jack rather than have him eyeing them.

"I repaired the barn door for your grandmother twenty years ago," Jack said. "The building was sound then."

"You knew my grandmother?" Eugenie felt a prickling at the back of her throat. The connection to her grandmother was unsettling.

"Oh yes. She was good to me when I first came here back in '71." Jack poked around the stalls and ran his hand along the beams. He opened the storage cupboards, then reached in behind a levered hatch door. There, he located a false wall that protruded out from the support beams. Pulling the hatch door wide open, he peered in and crouched down to pull out a rifle.

"A Remington 700," he said. "I haven't seen one of these in a while." He turned to Eugenie. "This belong to you?"

"No. It must've been my grandmother's. I didn't even know that door was there."

"I can see Alice owning a gun," Jack said, "She probably knew how to shoot it, too."

"Yes, I imagine she could," Eugenie replied. She was watching him as he looked around, trying to place him in her grandmother's life. There was something familiar about him, but it was hard to place him amongst the people who frequented the farm back then. "How did you come to know my grandmother?"

Jack glanced over to Dean then back to Eugenie. "I was escaping Vietnam. Your grandmother hated the war and sometimes needed a hand around here." Jack paused. "Well, she didn't always need a hand. Sometimes she needed someone to talk to."

"I think I remember that. I think I remember you coming here, my grandmother talking to you about the war." It was his voice that she'd heard before. Listening through floorboards, from inside the house, a faint recollection forming. They walked back to the truck, Eugenie anxious to see him off.

"In any case, check around. Lots of barns around these parts have false walls," Jack said. He looked at Dean as he climbed into the cab. "Some people too. Well, you know where to reach me should you ever need a hand."

They watched as he drove down the lane, unable to take their eyes off the truck until it disappeared down the road.

Eugenie sat by the telephone waiting for Michael to call. It was early, the sun barely up, the light dispersed by a dense fog that meant her world had shrunk to a mere twenty yards or so. It was late August already, the diminishing days signalling a change in the air.

She roamed the kitchen thinking she ought to call him but instead she waited, stubbornly, for him to ring. It was Sunday, and she and Dean had agreed to spend the day alone. For her to appear at the camp with breakfast would be unexpected, though in truth this is what she wanted. These two distinct desires, to hear from her husband and to go to Dean, made her realize that she was doing what people do when they have an affair: she had been reduced to her urges.

The Remington 700 that had been hidden in the barn for so many years now rested by the front hall closet, unloaded, now a mere artifact. Jack's visit had got her thinking that, like that rifle, perhaps Dean didn't need to be as hidden as she'd previously thought. This region was built upon men like Jack and Dean. There were possibilities here for those who could find the right opening. She wondered whether Dean had considered this, that he might have a place here, that he might be able to contribute in some way.

If Dean wanted to come out in the open, if he wanted to stay, then life on the farm would grow immeasurably more complicated for her. His hiding meant that she didn't have to decide what to do about her feelings; the two of them could be content just as they were without commitment or plans, in limbo. But if he stayed, if she accepted him in her life, her marriage would have to end. She didn't know if any of them could survive that.

She could blame Michael for her affair, having abandoned their plans for his own. He'd left her alone, invited these decisions upon her. The last time she'd spoken to him he said he would be going to Granada, and she pictured him roaming the Alhambra, living his life exactly as he wanted it, and she felt rising resentment towards him. She thought about the time not long before she left Spain when they had spent the day in the city. They had gone because Michael needed to pick up some material and he suggested they visit the palace again. They thought a day out together would do them good. But when they approached the front gate and saw the queue of people, the row of buses out front, the shops selling little jewellery boxes, chess sets and other souvenirs only slimly reminiscent of what they would see inside, he suddenly became morose.

They walked the streets of the city, which felt like a form of self-inflicted punishment, the heat, the frustration only making his desperation worse. They knew that it would be months before they would see each other again and yet this day, which was meant to be perfect, was wearing them both down.

They trudged up a hilly road until they reached the upper part of the city and leaned against a tree that offered some relief from the sun. They stood there a very long time watching women returning from the shops, sweeping their front steps, washing windows, while men who were too old or infirm to work sat on benches nearby, smoking, talking or just staring into the day.

They drank from their water bottles and when some dribbled over Michael's chin, Eugenie gently wiped it with her hand. This gesture seemed a reminder of why they were there, a chance to be together, to reclaim lost ground in their relationship. He pulled his handkerchief from his pocket and dabbed the sweat from her face.

Moments later, against the glare of the sun, like a mirage, they spotted a café down one of the streets and quickly made their way to it. They collapsed into the chairs and gave their order for coffee. From where they sat they could see the palace, its red-tinged walls.

"Alhambra means 'the red one' because of the red clay bricks of the outer walls," Michael said as he picked at the tapas the waiter had delivered.

The fortress-like exterior belied the intricacy of the décor inside, where all the walls, columns, floors and fountains revealed a craftsmanship in marquetry that Michael could only hope to attain. They'd visited the palace several times and each time they went Michael chose one small section to study. This was the only way he could visit the palace, by reducing it to one man's work, one single design.

"Do you know what King Boabdil's mother said to him as they left for Africa?" Michael said. "'Weep now like a woman for this kingdom you failed to defend like a man.' That was the end of eight centuries of Muslim rule in Spain. They had just handed the key to Granada over to King Ferdinand and Queen Isabella, then Boabdil and his royal party rode south to the Alpujarras. At one point in the journey he turned around and, looking back at the Alhambra, he began to weep. That was when his mother rode up to him and said what she said. Since then, that spot has been called the Pass of the Moor's Sigh."

He fell into his well of regional history, and she listened to him, because she felt that they were losing ground and this was the only way to be near him. They finished their coffee, signalled the waiter for their bill, then stumbled as though waking from an unexpected slumber down the narrow road to their car. They

76

sat in the suffocating heat, driving out of the city slowly through the traffic.

"Let's go to the beach," Eugenie suggested, trying to find some energy in a day that was waning. Michael was so flushed from the heat it seemed as though he had sunstroke, his face red, the back of his hand offering little solace as he wiped his brow. "It will be good to go for a swim."

He drove too quickly and they made it to the beach in less than an hour. By the time they pulled into the parking lot Eugenie felt that she could fall asleep, but she forced herself out, at once relieved by the cooler Mediterranean air. They changed into their bathing suits and plunged into the sea, the explosion of cool water on their bodies leaving them shivering until they adjusted to it. They swam in tandem trying to get rid of the lethargy the day had brought them and when they stopped, they breathed in the salty air, their bodies leaning back into the waves, their legs brushing gently against each other.

Later, when they had rested a bit on the beach they walked to a seaside café, ate a late lunch of sardines and drank beer. They sat in silence looking at the water drifting back and forth. Eugenie watched a young boy who was fishing from a pile of boulders by the water's edge and this scene lulled her into a kind of trance so that she could forget that this day was anything other than one to relax, that their plans for leaving were straightforward and in order.

As they sat sipping their beers, Michael sat back in his chair looking a bit distracted as if gathering his thoughts.

"I see it now," he said, taking out his notebook. He flipped it open and started to make a rough sketch. "They have been too close together."

Eugenie was confused at first, his return to work too abrupt.

"I've been forcing it, forcing them—the medallions—to sit next to each other but the designs are unique. They haven't been made to fit together like a puzzle. They need space. They need to be connected by something more fluid than the rigid structure of a geometric design."

He clutched his notebook and began shading his drawings, giving them each a border, like a river that flowed around them. He smiled to himself as he did this and Eugenie realized that he was lost to this creative urge.

Eugenie had drained her beer and sat still for a little while longer, taking on this new acceptance. They had not had a day off together for a few weeks and it occurred to her that they had forgotten how to do it properly. She sat watching him work through his sketches, a hand reaching out to her every once in a while as though to check that she was still there. She looked out to the sea, to the boy who now carried his catch draped over his back and thought of King Boabdil and his long ride into exile.

∾

It was still dark out. Inside the sauna, the rowdy wind soughing through the trees made Dean anxious, brought on a sense of foreboding. It reminded him of the winds that blew over Iraq. The sharqi blew through in the spring, turning the desert into a wild sea of sand. In the summer, it was the shamal winds, which were also brutal, like a Maine blizzard. Dean found himself longing for the heat, the blistering heat that would leave his uniform soaked after a walk across the yard. Wringing out the sweat, the fabric marbleized with salt, stiff and smelling of ammonia.

At first light Dean emerged from the sauna, made a pot of coffee and went back inside. He looked at the things he'd taken from the workshop. The tools, sharp edged, made for precision cutting and delicate gouging. The glue, the bits of wood all spread out as if he were preparing for surgery. He picked up the plank he'd taken from the barn and laid it across his legs and got to work. He'd seen the work that Michael did, the geometric shaped discs, the images formed from contrasting woods and he thought he could try it for himself, something that would keep him occupied when he was alone. He sat there for nearly two hours, piecing together the wood fragments until the August sun was high enough to give warmth to the camp. Then he pushed the plank from his knees, slid it onto the bench and went out to make breakfast.

The summer had turned cool again, which prompted his plans to gather a store of wood, get the stove up and running, and insulate the sauna. He'd already built a fire pit with a brick encasement to help cook in inclement weather, creating a shelf for his gas stove and utensils. He'd chosen the area for the kitchen because of the natural overhang of spruce branches that would protect him when he was cooking, and he'd built a lean-to with boughs where he could sit away from the weather.

He walked to the farm to get the sled of canvas and rope that was piled with the hay he'd bundled in sheaves the day before, and began hauling it to the sauna. This took most of the morning so he stopped for lunch before he began stacking the hay around the base of the building. By this time he was spent, his body aching with exhaustion and he felt an agitation set in, the hard work pushing him to some mental limit, so he stopped for a cigarette.

His thoughts turned to what was before him—his future and the possibility of a fresh start—which made him feel even more agitated. He was overcome by a sense of darkness within, a profound weight that pulled him down, and the conclusion that he deserved nothing; even this home in the bush was too much for him. He paced around the camp until he could take no more of the trees, and then decided to walk back to the farmhouse. He and Eugenie were supposed to spend the day apart, but it seemed to him it was much easier to be alone in a house than in the woods. The isolation was getting to him.

"What's wrong?" Eugenie said when she saw him at her kitchen door. "You look like you've seen a ghost."

"Ghosts are all I have out there in the trees," he said.

"Come. We're going to town."

"Why? What's going on?"

"We can't isolate ourselves like this. It's not doing either of us any good. I need to buy soap, toothpaste. We can have lunch."

"Are you sure?"

"I'm sure I need toothpaste, and I'm sure you need a change of scenery. Now come on. I'm getting hungry."

As they drove into town, Eugenie gave him the rundown on the eating establishments, and Dean agreed to a family restaurant in the centre of town. He went off to the drugstore to get the list of supplies she gave him, plus a few things for himself, and Eugenie went to run some errands. They would meet at the restaurant in fifteen minutes.

When he arrived at the restaurant, Eugenie had already taken a corner booth at the back. He held the plastic bag up to her, as if it were a prize, and sat down to the coffee she'd ordered. She looked at his face, at the smile that seemed pasted on, a twitching in his left eye, and realized that he was frightened.

"I know this is hard," she said, taking his hand. "But you need to get out, do normal things like buy toothpaste and eat in a restaurant. How long can you go on living like this?"

"I don't know," he found himself saying, unsure of his answer. "I got the wood stove going. That will keep me warm once winter hits."

"It's not a life. I see you changing. Some days you're full of ideas, but others you're like a closed fist."

"I'm reading again." He pulled a tattered paperback out of his back pocket and set it on the table.

"*The Iliad*?" She held it up.

"It belonged to Nick." He'd told her about Nick before. They'd met during boot camp, that soul-destroying period that's supposed to be character building—barking commands, men grunting, sweating, shouting. And then there was Nick, calmly reading *The Iliad* on his bunk as if he wasn't surrounded by a racket that would wake the dead. Nick had joined up late too, so they were both older than the others. He was in the Reserves doing his Masters degree, his father had served in 'Nam as well. So, it seemed their friendship was destined.

The waitress came by and took their order, an interaction that didn't appear to be conspicuous to anyone but him.

"This book eases my mind out there in the sauna," Dean said, flipping through the pages. "In here, gods and men hang out together. A son should not become a greater hero than his father because if that were to happen it would upset the natural order of things. Everything has its place."

"Have you been thinking about your place in the world?" Eugenie said. "The things Jack said the other day made me think. It wouldn't be so hard for you here. But it would be for us."

81

He kneaded his temples. "It's easy for you to say that. You've got nothing to lose. I'm the one risking everything."

Eugenie wanted to say that she was risking her marriage, that she was knowingly protecting a deserter, and that she had taken risks just allowing herself to feel something for him but she saw that he was getting upset.

"Are you feeling okay?"

"Look, I'm sorry. I've got a headache coming on." He was starting to edge out of the booth. "Would you be disappointed if we asked for sandwiches to take away?"

She looked up, her smile collapsing. "No, of course that would be okay."

In the late afternoon heat they drove to the farm, and Dean walked back into the dark woods he both dreaded and had grown to need. His head was pulsating, and he didn't feel right. He fell into a deep and heavy sleep, so heavy in fact that when he woke hours later, the blackness in the sauna confused him and he felt claustrophobic, as if he were lost in a mine. This blackness, with no shadows, triggered a wave of panic and he sprung from his sleeping bag, his hands pushing against the sides until he began to see shapes, the layers of darkness gaining dimension. The sound of an owl offered a reminder of where he was.

He crouched, waiting. The silence hummed in his head until finally he opened the sauna door and peered out. A light was flickering past the clothesline.

He grabbed the freshly-hewn slingshot and a handful of rocks and peered outside, wishing for night-vision goggles. He leapt out into the open with his slingshot held out in front of him, whirling around the campsite taking aim at anything that might start the attack. He kicked over the stumps by the fire-pit and took cover behind a nearby tree, his eyes firm on the steady light by the sauna. He was wide awake now, his heart racing, his mind tracking the area around the light, looking for movement.

But there was nothing. Just the soft, steady light like that of a glow-worm on top of the woodpile. Dean watched it for a moment, then he ran and took cover by another tree, this one closer. It could be a trick, he knew. It could be a bomb, a surveillance camera, it could be any number of things that would end his life at the camp.

His eyes darting from treetop to the dense darkness of forest, the silence unnerving, his breathing raspy, sputtered.

"Come out, you bastard," he called as he looked at the woodpile, at the white radiance. He crept closer, squinting. Then he saw what it was.

Phosphorescence. A natural chemical reaction in the decaying wood. His father told him about seeing the phenomenon in the woods. Light without fire, something that becomes luminous without being ignited. A peaceful light that threatened no one. Dean dropped to his knees and watched its slumbering glow, mesmerised, until dawn appeared with its own beam, allowing him to fall back to sleep at last.

∾

The phone was ringing when Eugenie walked into the house. She dropped the bags onto the kitchen table and waited for it to stop and the answering machine to kick in. She listened to her sister Ivy's voice telling her that she was coming to visit, that'd she'd be there by the end of the week.

This she hadn't banked on. Ivy had told her she'd planned to come, but that was in the spring and they hadn't been in touch since. Her sister was always making empty promises to visit, all without ever making the slightest effort to do so. So why follow through for once now, Eugenie thought, just as she was well-deep into an affair with a man she could hardly explain to Ivy. She'd been looking for a way to slowly make more room for Dean here, room with her. Restless nights that had her staring out across the yard to the forest where Dean slept, thinking of ways to go to him, to be with him. The days together, working, planning, turning the place into something. Her world had grown so contained that she realized it had become unsustainable to any unexpected news. And now Ivy.

Eugenie paced the kitchen trying to think about how she could ward off her sister. She needed longer than a week. She'd tell Ivy she was sick. Or that there were electrical problems. Or that the septic tank was failing. This is what an affair does, she thought. It makes nothing of deception.

That night, with Dean in her bed once again, Eugenie couldn't sleep. They'd been talking about plans for the harvest, the things that would need doing around the place before winter, but Ivy's impending visit was on her mind.

"My sister's coming. She'll be here any day," she said finally.

"Here?"

"That's right. She grew up here with me, ran away as soon as she could. We haven't seen each other in years. Now all of a sudden she feels homesick."

"Have you spoken to her about…"

"No," she said, suddenly feeling very tired. "I'm not going to tell her if I don't have to. We'll just continue as we are, me the wife with an empty home and you the hired hand who disappears into the trees."

"Okay."

Eugenie wrapped her arms around him. "What are we going to do?"

"It'll be fine," he assured her. "I know how to hang back for a few days."

She took his hand and held it against her face. "It's hard to think of the future right now," she whispered. "Let's take it one day at a time."

"That's what they say when you're in recovery in the army," he replied, his eyes closed. "One day at a time."

"Maybe this is a kind of recovery."

"Living in the woods? A recovery? I don't even know what I'm recovering from."

Eugenie let her mind wander into the future. She imagined Michael's workshop as Dean's. It was a dangerous dream but she couldn't help but think these things in the middle of the night, warding off other nightmares, the ghost of her grandmother unable to leave her in peace. Eugenie thought of Dean crawling along the barn's roof, shoving off old shingles, breaking up bits of rotting wood underneath as he'd done earlier that day. There was no claim to the workshop, he was just doing his job, but still the image stayed with her. The roof should have been done when they renovated the inside of the building. She'd told Michael that he ought to get the outside structure secure before spending time and money on the inside. But he insisted on getting his workshop going so that he could start work straight away. Michael had become consumed by this new artistic urge that marquetry had given him, leaving everything else behind.

Lying there, Eugenie couldn't help but wonder how Michael saw their marriage, whether he laid awake in Spain, whether he even thought about their future together. During their last days in Spain, before she left for Canada, there were clues then, she now realized, signs that she should have heeded.

When they'd returned to Conchar after their day out to Granada, Michael had stayed up most of the night, a kind of artistic fervour taking hold. He'd gone to his mountain studio while Eugenie sat outside the house listening to the intermittent sounds of rushing water against the hourly peal of the church bell. When he hadn't returned by one in the morning Eugenie went to his studio and found him there shuffling the medallions around as if he were playing some ancient game of draughts of which only he knew the rules. She offered to make him tea, or to bring him some food but he dismissed her, pushing the medallions away, abandoning them for his sketchbook. She stood in the background watching him draw a small scale version, then shade the area around the medallions just as he'd talked about at the seaside café. After a few minutes she left him to his work and returned to the house.

At five, Eugenie woke to find that he had still not returned. She went back to his studio. Gently putting her hand on Michael's back just as the village cockerel sounded, Eugenie pulled his sketchbook out from under him as he lifted his head. Michael rubbed his face roughly with the palm of his hands. Despite his vague protests about continuing to work, Eugenie led him out of the studio with murmurs of mistakes that could be made in the shape he was in. So he gathered his drawings, locked the studio, and they trudged down the path.

Eugenie had felt a kind of anxiety about the state he was in, convinced that he was unwell, that she would soon be abandoning him and, that left to his own devices, he would falter somehow. Her mood was low as they descended the mountain, the realization that in a few days she would be thousands of miles away.

"I thought you'd had a breakthrough with your design?" she said.

"It's not so simple," he replied.

By the time they got back to the village she was no longer sure of anything. She was working through a plan that would have her staying longer, postponing her trip to Canada at least until he had finished this project.

"I could stay," she said, finally.

He stopped and looked at her as if he didn't know what she was saying. Then he moved closer to her, sweeping her hair from her face. He smiled, a weary smile, but it was enough to show Eugenie that perhaps there was nothing to worry about. It was the old Michael again, tired and deeply immersed in the work. There was nothing holding her back now. She would go. Make a start. Get their lives up and running.

The next two days while Eugenie finished packing, Michael would slip away to his studio every possible moment. They had somehow already left each other by then, her mind on the homestead, his on his work. On the day she left, they drove for two hours to the Malaga airport, the landscape wobbly with heat. She told him she was glad to be leaving, that she was looking forward to turning the homestead into a home and she saw in his face a kind of confused blankness that spoke of the uncertainty of their future.

Now here she was: the future, alone, or at least not with Michael, but with this man who, just the day before, had stood with her in the yard on a break from their work, and had taken her cup from her hands, and led her into the house, into the bedroom. They'd fallen asleep, a relaxed, indulgent nap and neither heard the neighbour drive up. When someone began banging on the door, Eugenie flew from her bed and scrambled into her clothes, barely making it downstairs to greet Neil, who was dropping off some organic fertilizer she'd ordered.

Eugenie could barely contain her breath as she spoke to him, so nervous that Dean might wake up and call to her, that Neil asked if she was all right.

"It's this summer heat," she complained. "I fell asleep. I feel a bit disoriented."

"It'll break soon enough. Every year it gets like this, stifling for much of August and then we get a big storm to end it. I don't imagine this year's any different."

Eugenie retreated to get her wallet, steadying herself while clutching the bills to pay him. Only when he'd left, did she see that her shirt was inside out.

∾

Having been to town once, Dean felt able to go again. This time he needed plastic wrapping for the hay that insulated the sauna, and he wanted to get some caulking to seal the cracks in the walls. Eugenie was encouraged when he told her.

"It'll be good for you to do something as normal as running an errand," she said. "Take the car."

"You sure? You don't need it?"

"I've got some things to finish up at the house. It's no trouble."

He drove too slowly, unused to being behind the wheel of a car, and was startled when a pick-up truck, then a car, passed him. Going to town with Eugenie, he'd felt protected, invisible almost, as she dealt with cashiers and waitresses. On his own, he felt disoriented and spent five minutes driving from one parking spot to the next before settling on the one behind the hardware store.

He sat in the car, organizing the money in his wallet, making sure he could pull out the few bills he needed quickly. He'd shaven that morning but his skin was reddened in places, a few nicks had left a trail of scabs on his jawline. When he was ready he pulled his ball cap on and walked slowly, his gait practiced to look casual.

Inside, he was startled to see how busy the place was. No one paid any attention to him; everyone else was absorbed in product details and purchases as Dean tentatively searched for his supplies. He was reading the caulking label, trying to figure out if it would perform under extreme cold, when he felt someone brush past him. He looked up and saw that it was Jack, the barn inspector, but he too was occupied with his own business and kept walking to the cash. Dean felt a hot flush go through him as he stared at the tube in his hands.

As Dean snuck over to the next aisle, he heard Jack speak to another customer about the renovation he was working on. Dean was overreacting, he knew. The chance encounter held no threat. More customers came in and the banter increased. Men were talking across aisles, asking questions of each other about family, work, comments about the weather, the need for rain. If this were back home, he imagined he could be part of it, have something to say.

After Dean had collected everything he needed, he began looking for the right moment to pay for his goods, a chance to time his manoeuvre between customers so there would be no waiting in line. Finally, there was a lull at the cash and he walked over, trying to hold his pace back. He rifled through his wallet, found the bills he needed and handed them to the cashier. He shoved the change in his pocket, grabbed his purchases and left the store. It wasn't until he was getting in the car that he saw Jack shoot his hand up in a wave as he walked to his truck, and the feeling of being caught so overwhelmed him he didn't return the wave until Jack was walking toward him.

"Afternoon. You're the guy working at the Waters farm, aren't you? Dean is it?"

"That's right." He accepted Jack's handshake.

"You're not from around here, are you?"

"No. Small place like this, it must be pretty obvious."

"You're from the States. Your accent gives you away."

"I am."

"What brings you up here?"

"Oh you know. Change of scenery mostly."

"You military? I know a military man when I see one."

"I had my turn, yeah."

"It's been a long time for me. Hey, how about coming out for a beer sometime?" He pointed to an unmarked building with a dog tied outside. "I go on Saturdays for a hot meal and a cold beer."

"I'll do that," said Dean, with no intention of doing so.

"See you around, Dean." Jack gave him a little salute and then walked back to his truck.

Dean drove out of town, accelerating once he'd passed the sign out on the main road. It was a fifteen-minute drive back to Eugenie's but he'd driven for thirty minutes before realizing he'd gone too far as he imagined himself driving into a freedom he could no longer define. He was hardly aware where he was when he finally stopped the car. He looked around at the overgrown lane he'd pulled into, at the weather-beaten house long abandoned that leaned heavily, as if pushed by a constant wind. In a year or two it would collapse into itself, the structure rotting completely. He sat there for a few moments and wondered what he could make of a place like that, if only the town would have him.

He put the car into reverse, backed out onto the road and headed to the farm.

∾

The mornings grew foggier, the nights beginning to cool just a little. Unable to sleep for more than a few hours, at dawn Eugenie decided to go explore a section of the property she hadn't yet visited. She'd awoken to a nightmare of her grandmother and could not risk going back to sleep. Feeling dazed in unfamiliar surroundings but grateful for the fresh air, she followed a rough trail through a hilly, winding end of the property. She thought about Dean back at the camp and wondered if he was awake yet. She realized she was beginning to get used to life as it was, with Dean on the homestead and Michael in Spain, that it had become almost normal. She was losing her bearings. *What am I doing what am I doing what am I doing?* She was uncovering a version of herself that she didn't recognize.

And then as if conjured from her thoughts Dean appeared, through a thicket of reedy bush.

"What are you doing out so early?" she said, startled.

"Setting traps. What brings you down this way?"

"Nothing. Walking."

"I'll walk with you." He strode up beside her, draped his arm around her shoulder. "I want to show you something. You've got a dead tree around here that could give you some trouble."

Dean cut a path through the bottlebrush grass. Once they reached the road, they followed it for another ten minutes. Eugenie knew the tree before Dean pointed it out, a great sprawling elm that was listing heavily towards the road. The tree stood like a cathedral, dwarfing everything around it. Eugenie touched its rough bark with the palm of her hand.

"What should we do?"

"Take it down."

"Can it wait?

"We can take it down or wait for a disaster to strike."

Eugenie sat down, leaning against the tree.

"I had a bad dream last night. I couldn't sleep," she confessed. "I can't think straight."

"I have bad dreams all the time. But that's all they are, dreams. They aren't real."

Dean took her by the hand and pulled her up. They began circling the tree, to assess the job before them. Further up the trunk, its branches were tattered, long dead, ripped by the wind or torn down by the ice. Its roots had come loose over time, he told her, and now it leaned dangerously toward the road, where it could one day cause an accident.

They started to walk back to the house, trudging through the forest for a while before cutting across the coppice towards the house. As they approached the house, Eugenie saw a woman with short red hair walking towards the barn.

"Who's that?" Dean asked.

"I don't know. Someone from the Department of Agriculture coming for an inspection?"

But as they got closer, Eugenie caught sight of her face. "Ivy?" she called out.

"Eugenie, there you are."

"I didn't recognize you." Eugenie stood back to take a good look at her sister.

"Oh I forgot, I cut my hair short."

"And went red," said Eugenie. "I wasn't expecting you today."

"It's the weekend. I said I'd be here by week's end."

"I thought you'd call ahead."

"I tried. You never answer your phone."

"Guess I've been out in the fields a lot."

"Who's your friend?" Ivy asked, looking Dean over with a curious smile.

"Friend?" repeated Eugenie, flustered. "Oh, this is Dean. He's helping around the farm. He was just showing me an old tree that needs to be taken down back there. Why don't we get you inside and settle you in, Ivy? You know your old room."

"I'll be off," Dean said, slipping away. "Will be in touch with a plan."

"Thanks," Eugenie said, already leading her sister to the house.

Inside, Eugenie listened to the heavy steps of her sister moving around the bedroom directly over the kitchen, a means of keeping track of her movements while she removed all traces of Dean in the house. The kettle whistled. She heard Ivy coming downstairs, her clunky sandals banging down the steps.

"Where's Michael?" Ivy asked as she entered the kitchen.

"Spain."

"Still? I thought he'd be back by now."

"He'll be back soon."

Ivy took the tea from Eugenie and sat down at the table. Eugenie began setting out toast, jam, some fruit.

"You must be tired."

"I'm tired all the time now." Ivy clasped her hands across her belly, and at that moment Eugenie realized why her sister had come to visit.

"How far along are you?"

"Almost four months." She spread jam across a piece of toast and then bit into it.

∽

Dean stepped outside into the brisk evening air, then went to the stream's edge and leaned down, spreading his hands across the bottom as it swept through his fingers. After a moment, he wrung his hands together and went to the rabbit that hung from the branch of a tree, skinned, waiting to be cooked for dinner. It was a good piece of meat. His traps were improving.

He was hungry. He lit the fire he'd gotten ready earlier, glad of his foresight, and squatted before it, blowing gently to urge it on. A small flame sprung up, then died. He blew harder, sending yesterday's ashes scattering.

He tried lighting it again but now his hand was shaking and he couldn't flick his lighter. His contentment from moments ago disappeared as he kneeled before the pile of useless logs. He stood up and kicked a piece of wood. It went flying, hitting the sauna wall. He looked at the rabbit and briefly thought about eating it raw, but knew he couldn't do it. He swung at a couple of branches then did some jumping jacks to warm up. Without thinking, he started running, feeling the branches scrape his jacket, leaves leaning with him as he dodged trees in the wilting light, doing laps around the camp until his legs ached. He stumbled back to the sauna, opened the door and slumped down on the bench. Feeling spent of his anger, Dean went outside to the fire pit, calmly pulled out his lighter and lit the kindling on the first attempt.

Before long the flames were shooting up and he felt his face scorching in the heat. He stayed close to the blaze, thinking back to those cold nights in Iraq when they'd light a fire in a barrel and stand around telling jokes, drinking. The tents nearby with more soldiers watching movies, playing video games, or lying on their cots listening to MP3 players pretending they were all alone. Dean had forgotten that feeling of being on his own in a crowd of soldiers. He'd had friends, but mostly it was too many people in too little a space.

Now Dean was out in the middle of nowhere, wishing he had someone to talk to. The flames had softened and most of the logs turned to coals. He got up to get the rabbit. He cut it down from the tree and shoved a metal wire through its body. He placed it over the fire. Sitting down, Dean lit a cigarette and took a long drag before turning it inward, pressing it against the inside of his arm. He felt his skin melt like the uniform in his dreams. Someone had told him that a soldier's uniform would melt if it caught fire and he'd held that image somewhere deep inside of him. He took a hard breath and leaned his head up to the speckled sky above, then pulled it away as his thoughts fell back to the night an insurgent had crossed the wire and entered their forward operating base. A soldier walking past the latrine spotted the insurgent creeping towards the mess tent. Then chaos. Dean was shouting, his gun aiming into the semi-darkness, trying to pick out the intruder. A flood of soldiers rushed in, swarming. The latrine pockmarked, the insurgent riddled, the soldiers a collection of manic, desperate men. Anger, frustration, guilt. Their security breached. Later, a return to the hum of the barracks, background noises of controlled explosions, Chinook helicopters landing every half hour, a faraway popping that might be a shooting all ignored because they felt protected within the wire.

Dean took the rabbit off the fire. After letting it cool, he bit in. Its flesh gamey, and succulent. The night was quiet beyond the chirping of crickets, the distant call of a bullfrog. Back in Iraq, in all that constant noise, inside the wire was the only place you could relax. Someone would tell them when to get down, take cover, grab their gun or run like hell. Until that happened, they could play cards, watch videos, or listen to their music. Some chose to sleep. The longer you slept, the less time you were awake, the less you were awake, the less time you spent in the war. It was a twisted strategy for coping, but it worked.

∾

"I wonder what Gran would say about a hired hand," said Ivy. She was standing at the window, observing Dean who was working on the roof of the workshop.

"She'd be fine as long as he wasn't a Communist," said Eugenie. She wondered instead what her grandmother would say about a war resister. Or what Ivy would say for that matter. It was past breakfast and there was work to be done, but she didn't want to leave her sister on her own. "Does it seem strange to be here?"

96

"Yes. I didn't think it would be, but now that I'm here, it doesn't feel at all how I remembered it."

"It was strange for me too. But I came round. Are you planning to stay long?"

"I don't know what I'm doing." Ivy rubbed her belly as if to calm it, even though she barely showed.

"And the father?"

"In Japan." She looked up at Eugenie. "This was not meant to happen. There was no possibility of staying. This is not a happily ever after love story."

"What does that mean?"

"It means a married man with grown children."

"Oh. When are you due?"

"Late January." Ivy looked to Eugenie, and then she turned back to the window. "You know that looks bad. Your husband in Spain and you've got some guy from who knows where working for you. I watched him leave last night. He just walked off into the woods. And this morning, he's back, no car in sight. What's with him?"

"He's just someone I hired to do some work."

"But you're alone here, in the middle of nowhere. People talk."

"What people? Who are you talking about? There is nothing for people to talk about. I live here on my own, my husband is in Spain. I hired someone to help out. There is nothing to talk about."

"Remember when Gran had the accident and neighbours came to the house with food for us, everyone around trying to console her. I went upstairs to get away from them but as I was leaving I heard one woman talking about Gran and that young man who kept visiting, the one from the US. No one

97

wanted to say what they later found out to be true, that he was one of those who crossed the border to escape Vietnam. All the neighbours talked about was the impropriety of it. Gran alone with him."

"A town with secrets likes to talk."

"What does that mean?"

"People should mind their own business. Would it have been better if they knew he was a draft dodger? Would it have been so terrible if the town knew that he was running from war?"

"What's going on, Eugenie?"

Eugenie closed her eyes and let out a sigh. "Dean. He's a deserter."

"A deserter of what?"

"The Iraq war. He left the US Army, crossed into Canada and now he's living on the property."

The room went quiet for a moment.

"What are you doing?" Ivy said, finally. "You know they don't look upon that as casually as they once did."

Eugenie pictured the look of surprise on Dean's face if he knew what she'd done. She imagined him shaving by the stream, his face streaked with soap, her telling him that she'd betrayed him.

"Have you talked to him about it?" Ivy asked.

"Yes."

"And he just told you?"

Eugenie told her sister about the afternoon she got caught following him into the woods all those weeks ago. She would have liked to tell Ivy the whole truth, but she knew that confirming her sister's suspicions would only make matters worse. We are lovers, you know. We hold each other in the evenings,

98

against the cool, stark night. No, telling her that Dean was a deserter was a controlled detonation. There were too many secrets floating around to keep track of, and so letting that one go lightened the load considerably. "That man Gran had around. Do you remember him?"

"Not really. By the time we came, he didn't come around as much."

"His name is Jack."

"Jack?"

"Jack Butler. He still lives around here. He came to inspect the barn, and he seemed to remember the place well. He met Dean too."

"Does he know that Dean is a deserter?"

"I never said anything, and he didn't ask. But Jack's been around long enough, he may figure it out."

Ivy looked out the window at Dean climbing down from the roof. "This explains why you looked so jittery when I showed up. And I thought my life was complicated."

∽

Dean's hands were working the sander across the door that lay flat across two sawhorses, but his thoughts were somewhere in the Iraqi desert. Back and forth, pushing his ghosts along. The screen door of the house slammed shut. Jarred from his memories, he looked up to see Ivy out in the yard. Life on the farm had changed these past days since she'd arrived. They'd had privacy, and freedom. But now he was locked into playing the role of the handyman. Dean looked up from his work and saw no one. He was beginning to think Ivy had gone back inside when she'd appeared in the doorway, startling him.

"It's just me," Ivy said, stepping into the barn and looking around. "What are you working on?"

"Fixing this door," Dean said, trying to concentrate on his work.

"Eugenie's lucky to have found someone like you to help her out around here. It's so run down."

"The timing worked out for both of us, I suppose."

"You're not from around here, are you?"

"I came up from Maine not too long ago."

"That's right. Jack Butler told me as much when I ran into him in town yesterday. You know Jack?" Ivy said, watching Dean carefully. "He said he'd been out to check out the barn. He said he'd met you."

Dean let the sander rest. "Sure."

"He's from Maine, too. Been here a long time, ever since we were girls. I remember him coming to see my grandmother. He'd visit and they'd talk for hours. He came up in the early seventies with the rest of the draft dodgers and never left. You know about the draft dodgers up here. So many of them." Ivy walked around the barn, checking out some of the cupboards. "Times have changed though. A different war and a whole new attitude. It's hard to imagine what would happen to people like Jack now.

"It's hard to say," Dean said, his head bent over the door.

"Anyways," Ivy said, "Jack says he's glad to know there's another American around." She left the barn and Dean watched her get into her car and drive away. He wished she would keep on driving until she was back in Montreal.

The next day was Saturday and with Ivy around Dean decided to borrow Eugenie's car and take Jack up on his offer to meet him at the local bar. He could handle that much, he thought. It

100

would be good to talk to Jack, and maybe being seen with him wouldn't be a bad thing. He found Jack seated at a table in the back corner, overlooking an old jukebox.

"Dean," called Jack, rising from his chair to greet him with a firm handshake. "Glad you could make it."

Jack ordered Dean a beer and recommended the daily special. Dean was glad for the dim lighting, the corner location, a vantage point that meant he could keep an eye on the door and the other patrons. Jack was talking to him, asking him how long he'd been working for Eugenie.

"Her grandmother was something else. But she was good to me." Jack talked about how he'd come to see this town as home, that he'd married a local woman and they'd had a decent life until she died five years ago. "That's the first time I thought seriously about going back. I'd lived here most of my adult life, and with her gone and no kids there was nothing stopping me. I'm allowed to go to the States, and I go visit my family once in a while but it's still with me, that feeling when I cross the border, that I'm going to get caught." He looked at Dean, pausing before continuing. "I'm settled here, though. I don't want to go back." He laughed as he took a swill of beer. "Even if they begged me."

Dean was happy to listen to Jack and soon they fell into a conversation about Jack's work. For a while he could fool himself into thinking it was like being back home for a Saturday night, having beers at the local bar. He was happy to sit around and listen to someone else's voice instead of to the ghosts that invaded his thoughts back at the camp.

"They're calling for a big storm coming this way," Jack said when they'd finished their dinner. "Bigger than usual though. Gale force winds."

"There's a big elm over on Eugenie's property that might not make it," said Dean.

"You mean that one that's been hanging over the side road for months?" said Jack.

"That's the one."

"That tree died a long time ago," said Jack. "I should have mentioned that to her. That property's been so neglected. I'm sure it's been hard for her to know where to start."

"I took her out to see it the other day," said Dean. "It's going to clog up that road or even hurt someone if it comes down. I'd like to take it down, but it's too big a job for one man."

"I can help," said Jack. "I've got someone who helps out when I've got big jobs. I'll give him a call. "

Jack said he'd be there first thing Monday to help Dean cut down the tree.

∾

They woke to a muggy September morning. The atmosphere was thick with rain that had not yet fallen, the day increasingly steamy, as the humidity peaked in preparation for the storm. It had not rained in weeks and Eugenie's legs brushed against the harsh patches of thistles, as she swept across the brittle bush. The trail narrowed and she moved more carefully, watchful of unexpected dips or tussocks that might trip her, while Ivy followed with the picnic basket. When they reached the clearing Eugenie stopped and wiped her brow with her sleeve. She looked over at Dean, who stood next to the elm tree with Jack and another man she'd seen in town but didn't know by name.

"We've brought food," she called out.

"You remember Jack," said Dean, gesturing. "This is Brett."

"Thanks for coming. We're glad for the extra help."

The sprawling elm leaned across the road, its branches reaching out like great witchy fingers. Twigs laden with leaves swung out above the asphalt, waving in the breeze. The listing tree seemed intent on ruining the symmetry of the more obedient pines that surrounded it. Eugenie watched Dean and the two other men circle the tree and plan. He took a hunting knife from its sheath and threw it against the elm, then pulled the knife out and repeated the exercise three more times. He was talking to the men as he did this, as if this was part of the ritual in felling the tree. It was good to see him around other people, Eugenie thought. He looked different than before, like he could belong.

The wind blew up and Eugenie, hair fluttering in her face, looked up at the manic sway of treetops. They hardly got thunderstorms in this area so she never knew what to expect. She recalled how she and Ivy used to cower in their bedroom as the lightning cracked the sky when they were girls.

Dean and Jack were fastening a rope around the chainsaw. He had rigged up a harness and put it around his waist.

"We'd better get started," said Brett.

Dean pulled the harness over his shoulder and tied the chainsaw to a rope. He went to the tree and tested the strength of a few lower branches, trying to find a place to start. As he began his ascent up the tree, Jack and Brett held firm to the other end of the rope.

"I'll cut a few branches first," Dean called down. "Stand over there where I can see you."

He climbed midway up and started cutting away. He hoisted himself into position, found a foothold and scrambled through the branches. Once he was stable, he pulled the chainsaw up.

He tied the rope around a branch, then swung the rope over a higher branch, making a simple pulley with which Jack and Brett could carefully lower the branches.

Eugenie and Ivy surveyed the work from off to the side.

"Do you think they know about Dean?" Ivy whispered.

"If they do, I'm sure they don't want to make anything of it," said Eugenie.

The storm was blowing in from the east. It was scheduled to arrive by evening, but already the sky dipped down, the clouds gathered in bunches tinted grey, charcoal, teal, and amber. The colour of bruises.

The chainsaw banged gently against the tree, as Dean moved to another branch. When he pulled the cord, the blast of the machine tore through the woods. The grinding of the chainsaw went on for several minutes, like some great animal gnawing at the tree, working at a large branch that sagged heavily towards the road.

In a slow gentle motion, the end of the branch dropped down, leaving it hanging upside down. Dean shifted his angle to cut the tendons of wood that would release the branch, and it fell noiselessly against the din. Dean cut the motor and looked over to Ivy and Eugenie, as if to say, "Now we're getting somewhere". He appeared happy up there, like a boy. The wind sifted through the leaves, bending the long grass where they stood.

"Drag it off to the side," he called down to Jack.

Eugenie looked up to Dean, who had shimmied his way over to another branch. He began cutting the next branch, working quickly with one eye to the sky. The wind started to thrash around, which made a hard job harder. They continued for an hour, one by one the limbs falling, the tree left with little dignity as it became misshapen.

Then in a flash, the sky rumbled and the wind shot through the trees like a train out of control. They felt a shuddering, then a calm. It was hard to tell which was worse.

"We'd better pack up," Jack called up to Dean. "It's coming fast."

"I can get one more," Dean called back.

The rain seemed to be all around them but unable to fall. The wind buffeted and swooped up to nudge the elm tree, which creaked heavily so that the branches nearly touched the road.

"Come down now, Dean!" Jack called again.

A last branch fell, practically carried onto the road by the wind. "I'm coming down," he called back.

Huge pellets of rain began to fall as the sky darkened to night. A boom of thunder split the day open and Eugenie felt it in her core, staggering from the intensity, the compression making it feel like a bomb had gone off. The rain pelted down, sluicing off trees, sliding off her gritty skin. The hail was next, balls that felt like bullets, a full assault.

Amidst the onslaught, Dean was struggling to climb down the tree. The ropes were getting tangled in the remaining branches, and the wind was making it impossible to untie them.

"Run to the barn!" Eugenie shouted at Ivy. Ivy ran toward the farm with arms spread wide to keep her balance, looking over her shoulder to see if the others were behind her.

Eugenie stumbled over rain-slick grass to where the men were trying to find a way to untangle Dean. The sky lit up again and a few seconds later thunder pounded against their eardrums, and a crack so loud they all stopped, crouching in fear.

"I'll have to wait it out!" Dean shouted down. "It's too dangerous for you to be here. Go to shelter."

The wind gusted with such strength that Eugenie fell to her

knees. They heard a guttural crack and saw that the trunk of the tree was splitting.

"Dean!" Eugenie called.

"Back away!" Jack shouted pulling her away from the tree. "It's giving."

Within moments, the tree crashed down onto the road with Dean tangled in its branches.

"Oh my God," Eugenie cried.

They saw Dean moving among the branches.

"Let's get him cut out," Jack ordered.

The two men cut through the branches with furious urgency as they tried to get to Dean. The ropes had twisted around his arm, which had bent in an unnatural direction. He screamed as they cut him loose.

"Easy," said Jack. "It's probably broken."

Through the sheets of rain and wind, they managed to carry him through the brush and back to the farm. When they reached the barn, they were sucking air as they tumbled through the door. Inside, midday resembled dusk. Eugenie stood, her clothes stuck to her wet skin, her hair splattered across her face. The men set Dean down on the floor.

"We've got to get that arm free," Jack said. "Eugenie, do you have scissors?"

"Yes, in the kitchen." She ran to get them.

When she returned, Jack stripped the sleeve from Dean's shirt to reveal a deeply bruised shoulder.

"Well, the good news is it doesn't look broken. But it's badly beat up. We need to get him to a doctor."

"No," stammered Dean through clenched teeth. "No doctors."

"There's nothing we can do right now," Eugenie said, looking outside. She kneeled next to Dean. "Close your eyes. Take deep breaths. We'll get you fixed up once this is over."

They were silent for a few minutes listening to the storm pass, the sound of rainwater spilling from the eavestrough. For half an hour the thunder threatened to break everything in half. And then it subsided just as quickly as it had arrived, and the sky brightened.

Jack and Brett had to check on their own homes. "I know what he's thinking," Jack said to Eugenie as he was leaving, "but don't listen to him. It may not be broken but an injury like that can kill a man any number of ways. Internal bleeding, infection, not set right. I know the doctor in town. I'll speak to him. Just make sure you get him there."

"I'll do my best," Eugenie said.

She watched as the truck drove away down her muddy drive.

Autumn

THE KITCHEN WAS FOULED WITH MUD and leaves and still the marble clouds threatened more storms.

It had taken days for Jack and a team of chainsaw-wielding men from the town to chew up the tree that had once lorded over the north corner of her property. The gash in the trunk had split the nearby saplings, and bushes were knocked over as though tramped by an unseen giant. Now there was a gaping hole in the sky where the tree once stood. A carcass of leaves and branches stretched across the road. But in that time the humidity had broken and all semblance of summer's last gasp had disappeared.

Dean had changed too. Refusing to see the doctor in town, he isolated himself in his sauna for two days. When he did reappear, he looked more worn by the solitude than his arm, though it was obvious he was too injured to work. Eugenie had rushed to him when she first caught him walking toward the farm, heading him off to the barn to avoid Ivy. He would frighten someone who didn't know him better. His body had acquired a musky smell and he had a glare in his eyes that bordered on delirium. When he showed her the brace he'd fixed to keep his arm in place, she felt something in her buckle, like the failure of a dream months in the making. She'd waited until Ivy had left for a doctor's appointment before taking him inside to bathe him.

"You need to see a doctor," she said as she re-strapped his arm to his body. "This is more than you or I can handle."

Dean rose from his chair, wincing as he shrugged on his coat. His face was flushed from the hot bath, and he swayed as if he were intoxicated. "I'm heading back," he said. "I'm so tired. I need to sleep."

This was not the man she had come to know these past months. The energy drained from him, and unable to focus as she spoke to him. The tree had knocked him hard, his body was failing him at the moment, but there was something else. It seemed his spirit had collapsed with the tree.

Eugenie packed some food and Dean returned to his camp. Left on her own, feeling more alone than she had in months she decided she needed to talk to Michael. She circled the yard, until she finally got him on the line.

"Listen, we have a problem with Dean." Eugenie closed her eyes and held the phone close, as if someone might be listening. "He's a deserter."

"What?" Michael sounded distracted. She heard the tap running, then heard him take a sip, remembering his way of pottering about when trying to work out a problem.

"A deserter. He left the US Army, crossed into Canada and now he's living on our property."

The telephone was quiet for a moment. Michael sighed. "Bloody hell," he said, finally. Then, "What do we do?"

"I don't know," replied Eugenie, on the edge of tears, suddenly angry that he didn't have any answers.

"Are you worried?"

"No," she lied. "Ivy's here now."

"Listen, maybe it's good that Ivy is there. At least you're not on your own."

"Michael, I'm fine with being alone. But we do have a marriage here."

"I know, I know. I'll be home in January. I promise."

"Now it's January. Since when?"

"I can't get back before then. The commission's been extended. The client's ordered more pieces. I can't say no."

Then he told her about the bog oak he'd ordered.

∾

Dean started working on the sauna wall at three in the morning. An owl had woken him, but to him it had sounded like something fierce. He'd wrestled free of his sleeping bag and stumbled out from the sauna so that he stood in the moonless night, shivering in his boxer shorts as he tried to figure out where he was.

He rubbed his shoulder, feeling the bones he knew were out of place. He may have dislocated it. In any case, he hoped he hadn't broken anything. Once he was fully awake, he wrestled with his jeans and a shirt and sat for a good twenty minutes in the darkness, waiting.

Only it didn't seem like twenty minutes, more like an instant. His body stiff, his mind groggy, he had no idea of how far into the night he had moved. He felt around for a flashlight and tied it to a nail overhead, then he went to his stash of glue and wood fragments, making his way along one wall of the sauna, gluing the pieces, most no bigger than a pea, one after another with no specific direction or shape. This was his version of marquetry, and it calmed him. He stopped only to have a smoke and it was then that he realized he'd stolen a man's wife and his art, and as such would win no awards for gallantry. He resumed work after only a few drags, letting the cigarette hang leisurely from his lips, squinting when its clouds got in his eyes.

The sun's first light signalled that his work was over. In a state of manic lethargy, he put the glue and wood aside and lay down on the bench, waiting for the sleep that was always so close by to come and claim him. He slept for two hours, and awoke to find the sun farther up the trees, the sound of a motor in the distance. Another disoriented awakening. This time he rose slowly, allowing his thoughts to get organised before his body switched into gear.

He wrapped the sleeping bag around his back and walked out of the sauna, following the sounds of the motor, which turned out to be an off-road four-wheeler. He soon found himself on the edge of the area where the tree had come down. He was dismayed by the devastation; the tree now gone, little trace left of its magnificence. He sat down on a log and looked at the emptiness, feeling as though he himself had been gouged. The dampness of the morning made his shoulder ache.

He was starving. He felt like he was starving all the time these days. A rabbit would have been a treat. But he didn't have the energy to hunt. He walked back to the camp, unsure what to do. The belt used to strap his arm to his body chafed as he started jogging on the spot to keep warm. Then a noise stopped him, and he crouched behind some bushes, listening to a rustle in the woods, the creaking of a tree, the soughing of the wind. It was hard to say what was out there. The leaves, turning shades of red, ochre, and yellow, shivered and fell from branches. In the distance he saw a figure moving through the understory, and he crouched lower, waiting. It was Eugenie.

"Oh my God," gasped Eugenie, her step quickening. "What's happened to you?"

Dean motioned for her to follow him inside. "It's getting cold. I couldn't light the fire."

She looked to the stove that had chunks of wood beside it, all too big to use as kindling. She took his axe and went outside and cut up pieces to get the fire going. When she came back in, he was crumpling bits of paper with one hand and shoving them into the stove. She threw the kindling in and they watched the fire take hold. Soon the sauna began to warm.

"I have to take you into town to get that shoulder looked at," Eugenie said. "It's not right for you to be out here in this condition. I can't have this on my conscience."

"I can't do it."

"I'll find out if our doctor can see you. I'll tell him you're visiting from the States. I want to help you."

"I'm not a fucking charity case."

"I can't take care of you, Dean. I can help you, but I can't take care of you." Eugenie reached out and took his hand, cupping it in hers. She pulled herself closer to him, stroked his cheek. "I want you to know I can't fix things. I can bring you food, give you shelter, love you. But I can't fix this situation without your help."

She combed her fingers through his hair, brushed a few crumbs that rested on his shirt. She adjusted his shirt around his arm. She didn't look at him when she did this, rather just fussed with him as if to bring some order. Dean shrugged her off and went to the stream. He struck match after match, dropping them into the water, watching as they floated away, bumping, cascading, swirling out of sight.

∾

How long had her sister and Dean been lovers, Ivy wondered as she saw Eugenie disappear into the woods at the edge of the field that morning. It was a hunch, but she was a naturally suspicious person and had learned to be watchful over the years. She'd known about her grandmother killing her cousin before Eugenie told her. How long, Ivy wanted to know. She got in the car to drive to her doctor's appointment. Going on five months, she figured. More than just a fleeting affair.

As she drove to town, Ivy contemplated whether she should confront her sister about her private life. She decided it would complicate things. Above all, she needed a home for her baby. Getting mixed up in Eugenie's affairs would only turn her sister against her. It always had in the past.

I can't go back, she'd told Eugenie when asked about Japan. The father was my boss at the school. He would be shamed. This seemed an archaic term, one from long ago or from a less progressive society, and yet on some level it was Ivy who felt shame, not for being pregnant but for letting it happen.

At least they had that in common now, the shame of their transgressions. Ivy was worried, but now felt sure this was the right thing to do. She would have the baby here, in this godforsaken New Brunswick hamlet where she had roots. Eugenie would have to let her stay, at least until the baby was born. It wouldn't be forever, Ivy had told her. That was when Eugenie's eyes shot off in the direction of the trail that Dean took through the woods each day, not even aware she had done so, and Ivy had pieced it all together.

"Stay as long as you like," Eugenie said.

"And what about Michael?" Ivy asked.

"What about Michael?" Eugenie blurted out and this, too,

told Ivy all she needed to know. She couldn't help but feel pity for her sister.

In town, Ivy parked in front of the doctor's office, the only one in town. Jack had said he'd talk to the doctor, and Ivy wondered what it was that he could say to him. Doctors were discreet, she knew, but this was a small town and she'd seen how a person's business became everyone's business.

She was called in for her examination, sat with her legs in the stirrups and watched the doctor apply gel to her womb for the ultrasound.

"There," he said presently. "See the head?"

Ivy craned to look. "Yes. Yes, I do."

"Do you want to know the sex?"

Ivy shook her head. "I'd rather wait."

"Well, everything looks fine," he said.

After Ivy had dressed and was preparing to leave, she asked, "I hear Jack Butler has done some renovations for you."

"Yes, he has," the doctor said.

"We were thinking of having him do some work for us. We had someone but he's been injured. Ex-military, like Jack. Maybe you've treated him."

"I'm not sure I have."

"He's not from around here, he's from the States, just passing through I think. How does that work, anyway, when you get patients from away?"

"I care for peoples' well-being. Anyone who walks in here can pay cash."

"I see."

Ivy booked another appointment and drove aimlessly for a while along the country roads before heading back to the farm.

She found a little antique market in the barn of a farmhouse and bought a rocking chair she could use for breastfeeding when the time came. The fibre rush seating was ripped in one corner. She could sit in it, but it sagged heavily on one side. The seller had some extra coils of fibre rush and an instruction booklet on how to replace the seating. The frame of the chair was oak and otherwise in good condition and the price was a steal. She would need something of her own in the house.

"I can fix it," she told Eugenie when she got home.

Her sister looked sceptical. "Since when are you the handy type?"

They'd got it out of the trunk and took it to the barn, where Ivy could fix the seating, then sand and stain it.

"How was the doctor's visit?" Eugenie asked once they were back in the kitchen.

"Good. Baby's fine. He asked if I wanted to know the sex, but I said no."

"I'd be too curious to hold out."

"Sometimes, it's better not to know everything," Ivy said, looking out the window to the woods.

Eugenie busied herself with the dishes in the sink.

"Anyways," said Ivy. "I was talking with the doctor about Jack helping with the tree and mentioned the accident."

"What?" Eugenie whirled around.

Ivy held her arm up. "I didn't say anything, just that Dean's not from here and was injured. He said he'd examine him and it's easiest just to pay cash. So it will be fine for Dean to go."

For a moment, Eugenie stood staring at her sister, her long steady breathing a signal that she was trying to control herself. Then she offered only a restrained, "That's good to know."

At least five months, Ivy thought, if not more.

Eugenie fastened Dean's seatbelt, then got behind the wheel. The car dipped in and out of potholes down the lane, forcing Dean to hold onto his arm, which was in a sling he'd fashioned to keep it from moving.

"You okay?" she asked when they reached the road. He nodded and looked out the window as she turned towards town.

It had taken two days of his wincing with each move to convince him that he needed to see a doctor. He was tapping his fingers against his knee again, a nervous tic she'd noticed of late. They talked little during the fifteen-minute drive to town, and when she pulled into the parking lot, she went through it with him again. He was a friend visiting from the States, he had no medical insurance, but could pay cash.

They walked into the office and sat between an elderly man and a woman with a toddler at her feet. The receptionist called Dean to the desk, asked questions about where he lived, but Eugenie couldn't figure out if this was just being friendly or if she needed it for official reasons. The woman tapped away on her computer, and finally stopped and told him he'd need to have an x-ray.

"The doctor needs to make sure nothing is broken," the receptionist said, handing him the paperwork for the clinic next door. In the waiting room there, they sat in front of a television set.

"I haven't watched one of these in ages," Dean said. It seemed to calm him. He sat watching the flickering news, a trio of icons showing sun, wind and rain in the forecast, a segment on the baseball scores. Then the nurse called his name and Dean jolted, as if from a trance. He hurried into the x-ray room.

Back in the doctor's waiting room they had another twenty-minute wait and when he was called in he looked to Eugenie, his face blanched so that she thought he might faint. He emerged a half hour later, his shoulder strapped and he was clutching a prescription. The receptionist gave Dean the bill, and he put a wad of bills on the counter with his good hand for her to pick through. The doctor came out and glanced over to Eugenie, a look that suggested he was going to come over and talk to her.

"You're from the Waters farm, aren't you?"

"That's right. Eugenie. It used to be my grandmother's place."

"Yes, I remember her. You've got a lot of work to do out there."

"Tell me about it."

"Jack Butler said he was helping you take down that big elm the day the storm hit." He glanced over to Dean who was stuffing the remaining bills in his pocket. "This is no coincidence that you're here with Dean."

"Jack said it would be okay to bring him here."

The doctor stepped closer and spoke quietly. "Jack was right in sending him here, but he's not able to take care of everything in these situations."

Eugenie looked at him, unsure what to say. She felt Dean's presence behind her and she turned to see that he seemed to be crumbling in some way, that he might run off, or faint, grab hold of her at any moment. She turned back to the doctor.

"Thanks for your time, Doctor. It's much appreciated."

"Make sure he takes it easy with that prescription. Painkillers can be powerful."

Eugenie helped Dean with his coat and they went outside. She led him back to the car, where he landed heavily onto the seat.

"What did he say in there?" she asked.

"That I better be more careful not to get hurt next time I take down a tree."

"He's right, I suppose."

"He knows. They all know. It's only a matter of time."

She took the prescription from his clutched fingers and left him there, his head against the rest, as she went to the pharmacy, worrying that her hopes of being discreet had failed.

∾

"I can't remember things," Dean confessed, smoking again. "I can't remember the missions I went on. It's so confusing. It's like it was all part of a movie I saw long ago and I'm only remembering a few key scenes. Except my memories don't seem to mean very much. Vague sounds and smells, a boy rescued in the middle of a desert, a woman chasing her son. I can't see the faces of the other soldiers. I only see their uniforms, not their faces. I think about carrying a gun. I feel the weight of it. I sometimes touch my body as I walk through the woods as if checking that I have my full armour on."

They were in Eugenie's room, having snuck up when Ivy went shopping. Dean held one hand to his head as if he was trying to recall something specific. Then he got out of bed and went to the window, watching a hawk overhead.

"The nightmares bring back images but the holes in these memories are where I live most days. I get through the day weaving through one hole, then when it feels like something is surfacing, I jump into another hole. How can I be here now and have been in that hell months ago? I wake up in the night and I'm back at the barracks. I can hear my buddies getting their gear on, I can hear someone shouting over the radio, I hear the helicopters, the blasts, the Humvees, and I can't figure out whether I'm in Iraq or still here in the woods."

"Maybe you need someone to talk to," Eugenie said.

He knew she was trying to calm him, that he might be scaring her, but something within him couldn't stop.

"I'm talking to you." He was suddenly agitated. "This is what's on my mind."

"Dean. That's not what I meant."

"Not what you meant?" He started pacing the room. "Okay, well what did you mean? We've got to wrap things up? Where do we start?"

Eugenie took him by the hand back to her bed and after he calmed down, they held each other and eventually drifted off only to be awakened by the car door slamming. Ivy was in the house before they realized what was going on. Eugenie jumped from the bed, threw on some clothes and went to the bathroom where she flushed the toilet and ran the water in the sink. When she went downstairs, Ivy glanced at her then looked to the ceiling, which told Eugenie that she knew Dean was upstairs.

∾

The oak rocking chair sat in the barn like a battered animal, sagging, faded. Ivy circled it, trying to figure out where to start, dismayed that she'd taken on a project just as her body was being taken over by the pregnancy.

Ivy went over to the workbench where Dean had set up his work station—Michael's work station really—and observed tools

122

spread across the surface, containers of nails and scraps of wood from the repair jobs he'd worked on. She poked around looking for a knife to cut away the fibre rush seating so she could get started on sanding the chair. There was a toolbox open with its trays removed and placed nearby on the table. Ivy began sorting through the tools, returning screwdrivers to one tray, placing the nails along the back of the workbench, the clamps and saws on the wall at the back.

Under one of the saws she spotted a notebook. She opened it but found no name, then flipped through the pages reading the snatches of text that appeared to be quotes from a book: *Here was a peerless warrior with a life unrelated to war, a loner and an outsider who could see in the collective military endeavor nothing that pertained to himself, the most poignantly moral of all heroes whose business was the daily hazard of war.*

"What are you doing?" Dean stood in the doorway. He came over and took the notebook from her. "That's not yours."

"What are *you* doing?" Ivy replied. "I found it on the workbench. I didn't know it was yours."

Dean placed the notebook into his pocket and surveyed the workbench that now was tidy, everything in place.

"I'm fixing the rocking chair," Ivy said finally. "I needed to use some tools and couldn't find anything so I just put things away. No harm done."

Dean kept looking at her, the veins in his forehead visible, his face afire.

"I'll work on the chair later," she said. "I'm too tired now anyway."

She walked to the barn door, relieved to be near an exit, and when she turned back she saw his eyes, desperate, glazed.

"Dean, are you okay?"

He pushed her out of the way and staggered out of the barn, across the yard to the trail that led to his camp, covering his eyes as if shielding himself from a torturous sun.

Even though Dean had gone for now, Ivy felt nervous on the farm all alone. Eugenie was in town to get canning supplies and wouldn't be back for another hour. Ivy went into the house and locked the door behind, then sat in the kitchen with a pot of tea, her eye on her grandmother's gun in the hall, wondering if she could bring herself to use it.

When her sister returned, she tried to open the door but couldn't. "Since when do we lock the door?" Eugenie said, once she was let in.

"Since I don't feel safe here," Ivy spit back.

"What on earth are you talking about?"

"Dean."

As soon as she said his name, Eugenie dropped her bags, her look full of worry.

"What happened?"

Ivy told her sister how Dean had acted strangely in the barn, getting upset with her for tidying the tools, then had what she called a 'vacant' look that had alarmed her and how he pushed her then ran off into the woods.

"He hasn't been sleeping well," Eugenie explained. "The pain in his shoulder increases at night when the force of his body presses against it in bed."

"That's a very intimate explanation for your handyman, don't you think?" Ivy said. "I'll just let you know that all this secrecy between you two is making this place unbearable."

"I hadn't expected you to invite yourself to live in my house like you had some land claim," Eugenie erupted.

Ivy looked at her sister with sudden malice, as if the very act of explaining her actions was a humiliation. "I have nowhere else to go," she said finally. "I'm pregnant, single, unemployed. Do you think I want to be the third wheel to your secret affair with a disturbed deserter? No, to be perfectly honest, I had always counted on you to make better decisions than me. I see now that things have changed."

To Ivy's surprise, the anger fell out Eugenie's eyes. It was as if the truth of the matter, once out in the open, had relieved them both of the act of lying.

"I wish Michael were here," Eugenie said. "I wish things hadn't changed, that we were still the people we were before his brother died. We were in England then, we had no intention of leaving. That should have been it for us. But then Michael's brother David was killed. He was bipolar. Michael had him do some work so he could keep an eye on him. But Michael didn't always have the patience to deal with David. No one could really, not all the time." She paused. "It was raining the night he died. I don't know what was said, but David left the workshop in a state. Angry or hurt, I don't know. And the rain. Terrible rain. He ran out of the workshop, spent the night in the streets. They found him the next day on the riverbank. He must have slipped in the mud and fallen in. Michael was going to open his own business in Southwold, making fine furniture, artisanal cabinetry. For a while he couldn't do anything after his brother's death. Then he discovered marquetry, and it was like new life poured into him. He found a way to get better without me, he left and I let him. I thought he'd see what I did for him, that he'd someday need the life we knew again, that it would count for something. I don't even know how I would leave him, now. He's been gone for so long now, what's to leave?"

They both sat down and, for a while, said nothing, letting their tea cool. The sun began to set.

∾

Dean got up at dawn to escape the dreams that disoriented him. He swallowed another painkiller and stumbled from his tent. After a run through the forest, he returned to the sauna where the tools were laid out. Glue, wood samples he'd shaped into birds or leaves, bones that he'd dried from the rabbits he'd caught then cut into dime-size chunks. This gave him the peace he needed after a wild night of restless sleep. The painkillers were working, but they made his dreams worse. The methodical gluing and placing gnawed away at the time and distracted his mind.

He worked at it for two hours, barely moving, as his mind wandered off to the war again. To the final roll call for MacCormack after the Humvee explosion. It was one memory that stuck.

Nick had said he didn't want to go, said he couldn't face it, but Dean was adamant. Memorial services were a tribute to fellow soldiers, but they were also under the order of the commanding officer. Attendance was mandatory.

Nick pontificated about how Achilles acted according to his own moral compass, but Dean was having none of it. It was disrespectful. It was an order. There were only so many battles he could take on. Finally Nick caved and they got there just as the service was getting underway. The music, the scriptures, the tribute, the meditation, and then the final roll call. The First Sergeant began calling out the names of each soldier who in turn responded. Then MacCormack's name was called out, the silence held, unbearable for those who knew him, and finally the response, a rifle shot in his honour. Dean glanced over to Nick whose stony face revealed nothing. The ceremony ended and Dean went to him, knocked him a bit with his shoulder, and Nick smiled and laughed as though someone had said something amusing.

"Another good service," he said and laughed again, but when Dean looked at his eyes he saw that there was no joy, no relief, just frantic exhaustion. Dean pulled his friend from the room and took him for a drink. He let him talk about Achilles, the gods who ruled their world, whether life was more precious than glory and whether they'd ever get to go home. They drank until they'd honoured MacCormack and Achilles and every fallen soldier in between and the next day Nick was in the sick bay with what he claimed was a flu, and what the medic figured was a hangover, and what Dean knew was the sickness of war.

Dean rose from his perch, stretched and wiped the glue from the knife and in so doing nicked the palm of his hand. He wrapped it with a rag before placing all the tools in a row and covering the wood and bone with a cloth. He didn't bother to look at the wall where he'd been working. Instead he walked out to the stream where he let his hand dangle in the water, trickles of blood weaving through the ripples. When his hand reddened from the cold, he strolled deeper into the woods, finally stopping at a birch tree, the tree of life, and pressed his hand against the bark. He stood there for a good five minutes peeling away some of the white outer layer and then returned to his camp where he put the kettle on, ate stale bread and boiled the bark to use as an antiseptic.

൶

Eugenie walked out to the light of the three o'clock moon. It was nearly full so she could see clear across the fields from the porch to a string of silhouetted trees that ran across the perimeter of her property. The wind was down so there was little movement in the trees and the quiet was so intense she worried she might wake Ivy as she stepped across the porch onto the pathway. She tried and failed to search for the autumn constellation Cassiopeia, and settled on the Big Dipper that sat low to the horizon. In the summer, she and Dean had spread a blanket out in a coppice, the night sky alive with light and they'd tried to find all the constellations they could remember, often making up their findings. He'd held her as they gazed at the same stars she'd seen from England and from Spain, the constellations that shifted according to season and hemisphere, and seeing them here, in the backwoods where she and Dean had escaped, gave her the feeling that she really could live a different life altogether.

Then he'd had the accident and everything had changed.

She tried to imagine what it would be like when Michael came back, to have him here to resume their marriage as if nothing had changed. But it had been so long she had trouble seeing herself as part of that union. She kept going over the memories of her last months with him in Spain, as if there was something she needed to construct from their past to make good of their future. She was thinking of their wedding day, married by the Registrar and then lunch at a nearby pub. She'd tripped on the way in and tore the hem of her dress and Michael had ordered drinks then slipped away to find a pin so her dress wouldn't snag. It was moments like this that she thought of now, moments when his attention turned to her in a way that was subtle and unexpected. It was this she missed more than anything, those little gestures that had gotten lost in their big plans.

This is what Dean had given her. Little gestures. It all added up to someone who had taken an interest in her, in a way her husband had not in a long time. It had been easier when he first arrived, before Ivy landed on the farm, before the tree felling. She and Dean had plans, they had seen each other as part of a future neither had considered. He told her she should study herbalism, make something of her ability to grow things. She could believe anything he said back then, because he'd been scared but not traumatized, on the run but not acting like a fugitive. At night, alone in her bed, her mind went over the things that Ivy told her; his abrupt temper, his thousand-yard stare, the way he sometimes appeared to be somewhere else altogether.

Yet he was starting to tell her about these frights, this thing that was happening to him, and this seemed like another layer of commitment, their ability to share and work through his situation. His kindness was still there too, that part of him she'd fallen in love with. Just yesterday, he'd placed the rocking chair Ivy was working on up on a table when he'd heard her complain about her back, and this morning he'd told Eugenie she needed to spend more time with Ivy, that he worried she was overdoing it. This is what brought her out to the stars, the confusion of it all, this and the conceit that if she stared long enough they may have answers to questions she had yet to form in her own mind.

∾

Dean was in a frenzy tightening the door hinges. He was going through each room and then working on the exterior doors. More than a week had passed since his visit to the doctor, and he knew he had to get back to work, he felt that the place was starting to come apart with him unable to work. He knew it was beginning to wear on Eugenie, her having to come to him, feed him, bathe him. His arm was feeling stronger, but he needed the pills to keep the pain at bay. He needed to be part of the upkeep like he'd promised, like he'd been paid for, so he started with the hinges, because they'd been bothering him lately, their looseness, the sagging doors, the whine of one that leaned too heavily when opened.

As he worked, Dean tried to recall the names of all the men in his platoon, testing his memory, which continued to operate like a shutter, exposing flash fragments of his life in Iraq. These fragments had been vague, dreamlike but now the images were coming more frequently, so that he was seeing the full reality of his life. He needed to remember more, to make sense of things, to connect those strands that seemed to drift like fronds in a river. That's why he decided to meet his memory halfway. Trying to gather the people from his past.

Jonze, McKenna, Spider. There was that kid from Indiana who told them he'd been shot by his father during an argument. There was Brooker from Brooklyn, the one they called Cowboy from Montana.

Brenner. McDougall. Jackson. Dean went through his list slowly, saying them out loud to better remember them as he continued with his work. He was methodical, taking each screw out, assessing whether it needed replacing, whether the wood was stripped, then putting it back in. He sat on the floor replacing the screws on the porch door hinge when he realized he wouldn't have enough to complete his job and would have to go into town for more. It had taken two days to do the house and he wanted to finish, so he left everything and went inside to get Eugenie's keys, left her a note, and drove into town still reciting the names as a mantra: Brenner, McDougall, Jackson.

At the hardware store he went to the bin with the screws and put a handful into a plastic bag, then went to the cash. He put the bag on the counter and only then, with the cashier staring at him, did he realize that he didn't have any money on him, that he had left without thinking of the need for his wallet, for cash, to pay for his purchase, and this realization made him feel like the attention was all on him. He glanced around to see if anyone else took notice of him, and shoved his hands into his pockets, his empty palms held out to the woman at the till whose expression he couldn't read. He muttered that he'd left his wallet at home but she appeared not to hear him, cocking her head forward as if to try and catch what he was saying, but he just shoved the bag aside and raced from the store, the drive home a blur.

Back at the farm he went straight to the sauna and sat inside with the door closed. He had no sense of time passing until he heard drops on the roof, a splatter of rain as it worked its way through the lacy covering of spruce. He looked out the window, surprised that it was almost dark. He checked his watch and saw that it was six-thirty already. The wind threw branches against the building and the rain was suddenly like dropped marbles on the roof. Dean stepped outside. The trees were slick, their colours blossomed by the dousing. He let the rain drip down his face, his clothes drenched. He was thinking of the rain in Iraq, great walls of rain that made for flash flooding. He remembered the splattered mud that later crusted his uniform and he remembered the day he and a few soldiers got carried away throwing mud balls at each other. They'd laughed at the game, the im-

131

pulsiveness, the slop, until later when they finally walked away, worn out and filthy, they became subdued, as if they'd been reprimanded by their CO for acting like children. But no one had bothered them. They'd just grown tired of the game at the same moment they tired of everything, the mud, the war, each other, life. They had showered and retreated to their bunks, wishing they were anywhere but there.

Dean stepped back into the sauna and noticed how calm he felt, and this worried him. He sat back down and thought of Jonze, McKenna, Spider, Brenner, McDougall, Jackson. And the rain. He remembered the rain.

∾

"You sound tired," said Eugenie.

"It's late," replied Michael.

"Have you started packing up the house?"

"Not yet. It's been intense here lately. It will be good to be there."

Eugenie put her coat on and walked out to the porch, which was bathed in the glow of a late day sun that crested across treetops and sand-coloured fields.

"Are you still there?" Michael's voice was brisk, anxious.

Eugenie turned to see Dean clearing the dishes from the table. He moved like a monk, the plates stacked soundlessly, the cutlery dipped into the water as if made of crystal.

"I'm here," she said.

"The studio's a mess. I'll have to sort it out before I go."

"Hmmm," Eugenie murmured. "It doesn't matter."

"What do you mean?"

"Nothing. Just let it go. The studio will be fine."

"How's Ivy?"

"Good. She's tired these days and busy nesting. She's fixing up a rocking chair."

"I thought she was just visiting."

"She's going to stay with us a while."

Eugenie wandered out to the front garden, her voice lowered as she watched a plane dart across the sky. It was warm for November, and through the open window she listened to the gentle clinks of Dean putting the dishes away, stealthily sliding one on top of the other, removing all evidence of their afternoon together.

Ivy would be home soon. She had gone to visit a teacher she used to work with. Eugenie and Dean had taken advantage of the time alone.

The screen door screeched open and she turned to see Dean. He stood there, waiting, and for a moment it seemed that the three of them, Michael so far away in Spain, and she and Dean here under the copper sky were part of something together, not at odds with each other but merely different parts of an intricate puzzle.

"Okay, it's late," Eugenie said finally.

"I'll see you soon."

Eugenie held the phone at her side. Dean came down off the porch.

"All evidence destroyed."

"Good work."

"How's your husband?"

"Don't be cruel. It's been a good day."

"It's been a good day."

They had coffee on the porch, bundled in warm coats, and

sat talking until it was dark, and when it was time to leave Dean lit a cigarette, the burning end like a firefly following him home.

∾

"Is that for me?" Dean called out the next morning, as Eugenie walked away from the bundle she'd left on a tree stump. He'd stepped out of the sauna, unnoticed and unheard, when he saw her coming down through the trees to his camp. He'd watched as she stumbled over a gnarly root, nearly dropping the package she was carrying under her arm. He waited for her to come closer, expecting her to go to his tent or to the sauna to look for him. Instead, she moved through the trees and up to the camp quietly, as if she didn't want to be seen.

"I didn't want to wake you," she said, walking back to him.

"Waking me would have been fine." He bent to kiss her, felt the coolness of her cheek, but also sensed restlessness in her, as if she were trying to wrestle free. "Are you expecting someone?" he asked, pulling back. Her body was unyielding, her eyes darting about as if she were under threat. The way of animals.

"We need to talk." Her voice low. He searched her face. "Ivy doesn't feel comfortable around you. She won't let it go."

"How?" He searched the trees beyond her.

"She seems to think you're not in control of yourself. That you have anger."

"But you told her that's not true?" He chewed his lip, waiting. The air was cool, and he wished he'd lit a fire, had had one blazing when she'd come, as if that would make a difference.

"You should eat," she said.

"I'll eat later," he said.

They stood looking at each other, their breathing quick and shallow. Then he listened as she talked about the research she'd done on soldiers who had gone AWOL, about how they'd been able to get help from organizations, people who found places for them to stay, homes, normal homes, and how there were applications he might make to stay permanently. The government was not sympathetic to deserters, but there were situations where the soldiers had been allowed to stay. She was frantic in her telling, the need to help him, to alleviate her own sense of helplessness that had become enmeshed with worry. He could see that in her face, as she tried to reason with him, or rid herself of him, convince him that there might be a rational solution.

He listened, feeling as though he was walking backwards into a dark hole. He let the words wash over him, felt a hollowing inside, trying to decipher whether this was Eugenie's way of moving towards him, deepening her commitment, or something else altogether. Either way it was too much to take in.

"Do you remember the story of Achilles and Patroclus?" Dean asked when she'd calmed down.

"Yes, you told me."

"I know."

"And Patroclus was killed."

"Yes, Patroclus was killed. Achilles sought revenge and became a crazy war machine, killing the Trojans by the dozens until he confronted Hector, the soldier who had killed Patroclus. He killed him then dragged his body around, a wild, mad act of revenge."

"Why are you telling me this?" Eugenie said.

"Because war fucks you up."

"Don't say that, Dean. You're scaring me."

135

He didn't mean to frighten her. But he saw, too late, that he had. She was trying, he knew, trying to bring him back to a place where he could wipe away the dust of war, as if it were a phase of his life that he was trying to get past. She didn't understand that it was not an adventure he'd experienced. It was his life now, it was part of him, like his arm was part of him, or his heart, his quickly beating heart.

He pulled her into him, whispered sorry, then told her he never wanted to frighten her. They'd get through this, he said. "I promise you."

He held her closer as she tried to pull away.

The morning after the first overnight frost was starkly clear. The sunlight's rise slowly pierced the kitchen. It was early, but Eugenie was smearing plaster on the wall, up and down, side to side. She stood back, looking at the wall. The hairline cracks, like brackets on either side of the doorframe in the kitchen, had caught her attention a few days ago. She noted how shabby they made the kitchen look, and she worried that the wall might be crumbling beneath the surface. She'd been up too early, unable to sleep again, and crept downstairs to start sanding and wiping the wall. By the time Ivy appeared, there was a fine layer of plaster dust all over.

"I wonder if I should have a home birth," Ivy mused. Her belly was getting big. It was time to start planning for the actual birth.

Eugenie wiped the hair from her eyes with her arm, the trowel still in her hand. "A home birth?"

"I don't like hospitals," Ivy continued. "I'm considering all my options."

"Ivy, be realistic. This is not the place for a home birth."

Eugenie opened the plaster and dipped the trowel in, scooping a little on the edge. She smeared it against the wall, wiping it awkwardly along the crack.

"It could be," Ivy said. She was looking out the back door, over to the barn where Dean was already caulking the windows. He'd been at it since dawn too, anxious to get the buildings sealed before the first snow. "Dean's working hard these days."

"He feels bad about the time he's taken off with his injury."

"What's he worried about, that you'll fire him?"

Eugenie looked at her and then went back to her work, not wanting to dignify that with an answer.

"In any case, I'm going to try to get my old job back." Ivy walked around the room, avoiding Eugenie's gaze. "And I was wondering if you might like to sell the place," she said finally.

"What do you mean?"

"I mean I'd like to buy it."

"Well," Eugenie began, but she could not go on. Instead, she began picking the hardened flecks of plaster from her hands. She rolled little white balls between her thumb and finger, then brushed the dusty crumbs into the garbage.

"It's been on my mind a while. You don't have to answer now obviously. Give yourself time to think it over." Ivy shoved her hands in her pockets, holding Eugenie's gaze all the while. "I thought, perhaps wrongly, that you might welcome this opportunity."

"I have no idea what would make you think that." The plaster was starting to dry as she worked it so, instead of making it seamless, it was lifting bits up, disrupting the surface, making things worse. "Damn," she muttered, dipping her finger into the

137

bucket to scoop up a bit more plaster. She worked it with two fingers until it was smooth.

"It just seems like a trap for you to be here. What with your husband over there," and here she nodded toward where Dean was working, "and all the stress of your secrets, I thought you'd want a way out."

The idea of selling, of giving up the place her grandmother had willed to her, was too much. "I don't see it that way at all. And you've got quite a bit of nerve to come in here and think of me like that. Is that the real reason you came back?"

"You know what's unfair," Ivy said. "That this place got left to you. That, once again, I wasn't even an afterthought in anyone's reckoning." She stormed back upstairs.

Still facing the wall, Eugenie closed her eyes and returned to thoughts of her grandmother. Why exactly had she left her the homestead, leaving nothing to Ivy? The question had always been there, under the surface, afraid to be answered. She knew her grandmother had been devastated by the accident that took away their parents, her daughter and son-in-law. Her grandmother had been left with two girls lost in their own grief, and this seemed to elevate the part of her personality that chafed against the outside world.

Eugenie was not meant to be home the day her grandmother ran over her cousin. Ivy had gone into town with a friend, and Eugenie had been invited. Then she'd got her period and decided to stay in bed with a hot water bottle. Her grandmother's cousin had come to borrow some tools. As Eugenie lay in bed, she heard strains of their argument in the yard amidst the opening of a trunk latch, tools tossed in, the intermittent sounds of someone rummaging in the workshop. The voices escalated. Eugenie rose from her bed and saw her grandmother getting into her truck, and the cousin kneeling behind a ride-on lawnmower that he was working on. He'd taken it out into the yard, pushed it out to get it started, and now it sat at the edge of the driveway, where her grandmother often backed her truck in order to drive down the lane.

The truck swung back, her grandmother's temper evident in her driving. Eugenie saw the cousin stand up, back away from the mower to assess his work. The two movements synchronized into a grotesque choreography of impact. Cousin fell away, his head against the lawnmower, grandmother jumping from the truck, silence blanketing the yard, everything at a standstill.

It was then that her grandmother looked around and saw Eugenie paralyzed at her bedroom window, an obvious witness. It was an accident, Eugenie knew, the argument unimportant, a regular spat they'd carried on for years, but she saw her grandmother's horror, and her fear. Eugenie knew this to be a responsibility she would carry with her always.

Not for the first time Eugenie felt the weight of the farm. How much work would it take to make it new again, to leave behind all that came before?

"I've invested too much to give this up." Eugenie was muttering to herself now as she scrubbed plaster dust off the floor. "I won't be manipulated. Even if she's having a baby."

She'd been telling herself that everything would be settled when Michael came home. They could make plans, think about what they really wanted, the burden of these last few years finally past them. This is what she told herself when she weeded her garden, when she painted her fence, when she plastered her walls. When Michael came home, their lives could finally break free from the homestead's history. But now it felt like she was just adding onto its past burdens rather than erasing them. No matter how much of a clean start she desired, the spirit of the place was proving difficult to change.

∾

He was high atop a cliff, the punishing wind flapping his coat as he watched a man running towards him. Nick. It was Nick.

Dean waved his arms wildly overhead, and an exhilarating rush of relief swamped him as he took off, stumbling along the cliff top. Nick was alive. He ran toward his old friend. But as Dean got closer, he saw that it wasn't Nick. It was a warrior, clad in an ancient uniform. He had been sent to bring Dean back to the war. "You're needed," he told Dean. Dean turned and tried to run away. But the warrior followed and gave chase along the cliff, the waves below gaining strength, both aware that a storm was brewing.

Dean shouted back at the warrior. "You must go back without me." The roar of the water below made it difficult to hear anything. "Patroclus, Patroclus." The warrior kept repeating the name, but Dean didn't understand. Then a wave like a rolling tsunami washed over them.

He woke up curled under a tree, with no memory of how he'd gotten there, clutching his sleeping bag. The moon was low in the sky. He lay accosted by the dream, until he was able to pull himself up against the tree. He had to shed its residue, so he quickly got to work in the sauna, tracing out lines that he would follow with glue, then overlay with wood or bone. His shoulder a distant thought, Dean took another painkiller. He ran his hand over the wall and he felt the design as best he could. This gave him some relief.

His mind entranced by his work, he slipped back into flickers of his dream. Had he really been atop that cliff? Had he really seen Nick? He felt the disappointment of something taken away, and his heart turned back into a weight, pulling him down. He rested his hand on the marquetry, wishing that Eugenie would come. But he knew that wouldn't happen. She had grown more anxious lately, and appeared colder to him. She seemed distracted with Ivy, and plans for the baby, an event designed to lock him out forever.

Ivy had been spying on him. Dean wondered if he should tell Eugenie. Sneaking up when he was working, appearing out of nowhere. Yesterday, she'd followed him into the woods when he was heading back to the sauna and then pretended she was just going for a walk. He sent her back, but not before scaring her into thinking there were bears in the woods, telling her he'd seen a big brown one a few days ago on his way to work. She'd asked about his uncle's cabin, trying to trick him, but he answered straight away, pointing off in a direction he thought was north, even naming a road that led to the cabin from the adjoining highway.

He'd been in top form, spinning a story about this particular uncle who married into the family. By the time Ivy turned back, he was sure he'd convinced her. Feeling strung out from the tension, he headed to the sauna and collapsed into a deep sleep, until darkness fell and he woke to a dream that took him to the top of a cliff.

~

A few days later, the weather cooled in its first indication that winter was unmistakably on its way. Eugenie drove Dean into town. The doctor wanted to see his shoulder again to make sure there were no problems. Eugenie convinced him it would look worse if they didn't show up, though she feared that the physical ailment was the lesser of his problems. As Eugenie drove, she listened to the rise and fall of his breathing, alert for agitation. She looked at the coarseness of his cheap cotton shirt, which she'd cleaned and ironed, noticed his hands, resting on his legs, chapped, red, papery fragments of glue here and there.

Eugenie pulled into the parking lot, and Dean let himself out of the car, walking ahead to the office. To her relief, he was calm and polite with the receptionist, who sent him for another x-ray. He paced the floor of the waiting room, and Eugenie tried to signal for him to sit down. He took long purposeful strides into the x-ray room when his name was called, and when he came out he went straight back into the doctor's office, barely looking at Eugenie as he walked past.

When he came out of the doctor's office, he was upset with her, she could tell. Keeping his mood swings at bay had become an exhausting and all-consuming task.

"I thought I could trust you?" he hissed. "He talked to me like I was a fugitive."

"I said nothing, Dean. Please calm down."

"Who then? Your sister. Who else could it be?"

"Dean, please." Other patients, she could sense, were quietly listening in. Eugenie led Dean outside by the arm.

"Someone's going to track me down," he shouted, once outside. "He can set a trace in his computer. He doesn't have to say anything."

"Dean, you're being paranoid. Please. Stop this."

"How can I? You're trying to get rid of me."

"I'm trying my best. You're scaring people."

"Michael's coming back soon, and it comes down to your secret or mine. I get it."

She began to cry as they drove.

"I'm sorry," he said, leaning against the windowpane. "That stressed me out, going there." He motioned back to the doctor's office. "I know you're trying to help. I'm trying to imagine a way out of this that has us together." His voice was low, and his hair had gone wild again from running his hand through it.

"I understand," she said, aware it sounded insincere. "This has been hard for you, I know. But the doctor said you're fine. Your shoulder is healing."

He sat back and closed his eyes, lost again to his own thoughts.

The next day, feeling that she needed answers that could help Dean plan a future, Eugenie went into town with the excuse of running more errands. Once there, she walked up the steps to the library, a century-old stone building, to use the one public computer that had access to the Internet. She needed to help Dean, she needed to find a solution that made sense. She needed to learn more about what it meant to be a deserter and what it would mean if Dean turned himself in.

After nearly two hours of online surfing, she was hardly any further ahead in knowing what to tell Dean. It seemed that the tide had turned in terms of how Canada treated the US deserters. Back during the Vietnam War, soldiers could count on full support when they crossed the border—in the ten years between 1965 and 1975 some fifty thousand soldiers took refuge in Canada and were quietly embraced by the country. This was the climate in which Jack had entered New Brunswick, but things had changed. In the first three years of the Iraq War, over twenty thousand had deserted, and several hundred of them had crossed into Canada hoping they would find the same kind of support. A change in government meant a change in ideology and policy, one that now had deportation as its main thrust. To desert in a time of war carried a maximum penalty of death. She doubted it would come to that, but the sight of the words disarmed her.

She sat down on the cold steps of the library and closed her eyes to the sun. The day had started out with a surge of clarity as she emerged from her sleep unburdened by the dreams that had been keeping her awake lately. Her thoughts had formed around the idea of pushing Dean to seek asylum. She would help him find a home. Together they would come up with a plan. There were ways, she'd seen herself explaining in a calming manner, there were always ways. But there were moments if she wondered if that were true.

∾

By the time December's wind chills started to come on strong, Dean had insulated his sauna, pioneer style, with hay bales at the outside base and straw packed into the walls he'd then covered with another layer of pine board. But he was still getting a draft inside. Dean pulled himself out of his sleeping bag and went out to search for the hole, but it was too dark. He stared at the gibbous moon, neither new nor full.

He was becoming a nighthawk. Awake at three, asleep by first light. He checked his watch and saw that it was just after two. Night stretched out before him, filling him with dread. He tried to read but the words were all jumbled across the page, his eyes unable to follow the thread.

After a time, he put the book aside, lay back in his tent and listened to the night sounds, thinking of another cold desert night when any sleep would have been a gift. It was hard to escape these night thoughts that crowded him, those that drifted back to the war. They hadn't expected any action as they'd just come off three days of heavy fighting and word from Intelligence was that the insurgents had suffered severe casualties. They were sitting on their bunks, Nick muttering about what they could do without for the next twenty-four hours if they had to: food, water or sleep. A conversation they could have only because they expected to have all three.

Then came word of a roadside bomb and increased fighting up in the mountains. They scrambled to rehydrate and ate three MREs before heading out. The night was clear, and Dean was pissed off to be sitting in the back of a Humvee, wedged in like a damn sardine, when he really wanted to be stretched out on his bed. They drove into the darkness, the radio intermittent with rasping updates until they saw the outline of the mountain. They reached the foothills, where they held up for the night, digging ranger graves where they would sleep, waiting for word, or the sound of war that would direct them to the next chain of events. Sleep was fitful, however, because of the brightness of the moon, the anticipation of battle, the exhaustion of the past days. Occasionally a rocket burst through the quiet night, making everyone jumpy.

Dean was in a dizzy half-sleep when someone started shouting. Exhausted, disoriented, he began scrambling around for his gear, his mind sluggish, his hands shaky as though he'd had too much caffeine. Somehow he got separated from Nick, who was ordered up the ridge with two others, sent to provide cover while the rest made a frontal attack. But he was too disconnected for it to register. Too much war had left him feeble. He'd been at it for weeks.

He followed the men into battle, on a rush of adrenaline, his gun positioned vaguely in the direction of the enemy, watching for flash fire, waiting for clues on where to shoot. It was a beautiful night, a blue-black sky and half-hearted moon, scarred by the fireworks of combat and confused by the shouting of men. There was something spectacular about a night sky in the midst of battle.

Dean perched against a boulder, the cold rough stone against his face, unable to see much beyond the flash of weaponry going off somewhere in the wilderness. He was breathing like a runner, taking deep, gasping breaths. He tried to regain some control. He wasn't anywhere near it.

Then explosions, shouting, soldiers rushing forward, a frenzied version of the games he'd played as a child, and Dean feeling the delirious thrill his father talked about, his heart pumping toward a heart attack. This was the splendour of war, the battle rush, the roller coaster, pumped up on all cylinders version of war, with the sky a magnificent stage production, all pyrotechnics, exploding across the wide open stage that had no visible limits. Guns and rockets were firing off around him, and he wore the mantle of a drunken man, all bravado, reckless, feeling he was invincible. He was running, running as he'd never done before, shooting into the night, soldiers left and right, fighting their own battles. It was superlative. It was like nothing he'd been through before. It was war. At its finest.

Then it was over. The quiet, sudden and stark, daunting. The silence itself was tangible, something of nothing. He crouched amidst the ready soldiers, the occasional rattle of a gun, the feeling of something draining away, as if he were being hollowed, a protective husk shrugged off, an emptiness that wouldn't let anything in. Dean stumbled back to his ranger grave, and within minutes he knew. Melanson creeping over to him, barely able to look at him, with words that could not form a sentence. Nick. Dead.

He thought of that moment now, lying in his sleeping bag under a great northern sky, as safe as a man could be. The moment when Melanson told him. *Scholes. Shot. Nick. He was talking about Nick.* Dean knew he was responsible. He'd gotten carried away with war. Thought himself invincible. He should have followed Nick up the ridge. To fight together, that's what friends did. Instead, Dean's fixation on not wanting to be there, for the battle to be over, had turned into something hyper-real. He'd begun fighting an exaggerated form of war, where no one got hurt, no one got killed. He'd fought as though he were alone out there, a mistake no soldier should make.

Dean had always been the better soldier. He had instincts. He saw things others didn't. Out in combat the men looked to Dean to see what they couldn't. The ridge was a vulnerable position. The insurgents knew the hills, knew where the soldiers would go for cover. They probably watched Nick and the others as they made their way up, waited until there was no turning back before they opened fire. That's what Dean would have done if the tables were turned. It was good tactical manoeuvres.

Dean could hear the freezing wind whistle as it filtered into the sauna from some unforeseen weakness in his design. Nick often told Dean that when he was waiting for battle, he would think of the Trojan War, to remind him that others had been there before him, that other men had fought wars. It gave him courage. It was hard not to think of the story of Achilles now. Of the reluctant soldier, with the golden gift of fighting. Nick, his constant friend, had saved him from slipping too far into himself, had given him the joy of camaraderie, the relief of kinship. He had been his Patroclus, loyal, patient, mindful of his needs. And now he was dead.

∾

The wind howled all day, whipping up an atmosphere that would bring on the first snow set for later in the evening. It was late this year, nearly Christmas and not a snowflake to be seen.

The canning had been done, the storm windows installed, the garden covered with straw and Ivy was still considering whether she could brave a home birth when her water broke. The snow was just getting started, sweeping across the road like dust, not yet sticking to anything. Eugenie was preparing dinner, when Ivy walked into the kitchen, her pants drenched. It was over a month before her due date but the baby would not wait. They packed a suitcase and headed to the hospital, the whirl of snow mesmerizing the darkness. They rushed into a room, and Ivy was told that the baby was ready but her body was not. So they waited.

It took till noon the next day for Ivy to give birth. By then, the snow had transformed windows into portholes and built surf-like crests that rose to a foot or more across town and out in the country. She named the baby Alice, after her grandmother.

Winter

EUGENIE STOOD AT THE WINDOW that looked out onto the runways. She was early and each plane that landed was like another false homecoming. A silver fleck in the sky would catch her eye, eventually materializing into an airplane, her pulse quickening with expectation, as she worked through her rehearsal of Michael's arrival. She'd gone through it a dozen times or more, that moment he would walk through the gate. She'd smile and wave, and she'd think to herself how glad she was to see him, because that's how she would need to be when he finally reached her, when he pulled her into an embrace.

She checked her watch. Another forty minutes. She pictured him packing up his book, having that last drink of water, perhaps finishing his beer while looking down over the landscape of snow-dusted trees that stretched for miles, broken only by the occasional frozen pond or lake, a river coiling through the sprawling white forest. She knew this landing well. Slowly descending, the textured landscape below empty, with no sign of an airport or any form of civilization until they were moments from touchdown.

In their last conversation, he told her that the commission was on hold and he would be leaving in two days. There was a manic agitation to his voice, the excitement of getting so close, the answer finally found in the use of bog oak, the frustration of having to wait.

"Domenico di Niccolò," he'd practically shouted into the telephone. "He was an Italian from the early fifteenth century who discovered he could make the marquetry bolder by the use of black wood as a background." Michael had explained how di Niccolò used bog oak, the wood from a submerged oak tree that caused the water to react with the tannic acid, turning the fibre dark. The longer the wood stayed in water, the darker it would be. It could take centuries for the oak to fully blacken, but exposed to air it wouldn't rot.

Eugenie had listened, thinking of the swampy tracts of her land where trees stood branchless, their scrawny trunks stripped of bark, slowly drowning. There was something brutally serene about these scenes. She wanted to tell Michael about the trees, thinking for a moment it might be useful to him, that he could use the submerged wood they had available to them. But he had moved on in the conversation, talking about his customer, and how he wished he could just get on with the work.

Eugenie checked her watch again before walking over to the arrivals screen. New York, his stopover. On time. Seven minutes. She went back to the window and scanned the sky, searching for a fleck of metal that would deliver Michael. Such was her concentration that when the airplane appeared from the other direction, its wheels touched the runway before she realised he'd landed.

She watched the airplane taxi to the loading bridge, the portal to their reunion, thinking of her own journey from Spain almost two years ago. Arriving after the eight-hour flight, the plane buffeting as it neared the runway and Eugenie gripping the chair's arms, suddenly frightened by everything that lay ahead. Then came the bounce when it landed, a jolt into her own future. Outside, the filmy heat of Spain long gone, she stepped from the plane into the loading bridge, where the air was crisp, a tangible difference between here and there. Everything was about abrupt change back then, as though she had to shock herself into moving in a new direction.

Eugenie left her post at the window and made her way down to arrivals, thinking of Michael, of his renewed enthusiasm for his work. Twenty minutes passed and she felt a rising anxiety, wondering if he might have missed his plane. Finally she spotted him guiding his suitcase around a slow-moving family. She caught his eye and offered a smile, a small wave. Someone bumped into him and he turned to pull his suitcase out of the way. By the time he started walking again, Eugenie was in his arms.

"Michael."

She held him close as though she meant it, and in that moment she did mean it—she had missed him. Her own feelings of guilt pushed aside for the moment, she held Michael and wondered if they could ever go back to how things once were, when they were still planning for this future at the farm, rather than living an errant version of it.

"How are you, love?"

"Better now."

"How's Ivy? The baby?"

"Noisy. Chaotic. Beautiful. Charming."

"Which one?"

She looked at him, smiling. "The baby." They walked to the door while Eugenie filled him in on the baby's impact on both the household and on Ivy, whose maternal instinct had surprised Eugenie. "She won't let me help. She's determined to do this on her own."

There was a time Eugenie thought she and Michael would have children, but medical tests determined her hormone levels would make that possibility unlikely. It was a subject they'd long since packed away.

"And are you coping?" Michael asked, still looking at her. "You've lost weight."

"Wait till you see the place. We've been working hard." She'd made an agreement with a local farmer to rent out her fields this coming spring and, with plans for the greenhouse underway, the next season's activities were already mapped out. This is what she wanted to say to Michael most of all, that she had done it. That the farm was working out. Instead she handed him the winter coat she'd brought him and got behind the driver's seat for the long drive back.

∞

Dean was out on his morning patrol, the branches whooshing past him, leaving a trail of fluttering snow. The trees had crystallized in the overnight frost. A blade of sunlight streaked through the forest. Stopping to catch his breath and check his pulse, he took a drink of water and looked around at the sudden brilliance of his surroundings. That's when he saw Michael and Eugenie walking along the trail that led to the house.

The clattering of ice falling from the trees caught their attention. They both turned and spotted Dean. Michael made the first move, walking towards Dean in the way of a landowner.

"Dean, this is Michael." Eugenie trotted ahead to make the introduction, standing between the two men. "Michael," she gestured. "Dean."

"It's early. What brings you out?" Dean said as he gave a quick nod. He strained to keep his voice calm.

"I couldn't sleep," Michael said. He rubbed his face roughly with his hands and looked around at the woods. "Jet lag."

Dean eyed him, thinking of the camp. If Michael were to start his day tramping through the woods, he'd eventually find his camp. In the sauna, he would find the tools and supplies he'd stolen.

"Do you live nearby?" Michael asked.

"Not far. My uncle has a camp." Dean gestured vaguely in a direction opposite to the house. He followed Michael's gaze, seeing the forest through his eyes, the wild unruly growth, the soaring trees and unkempt underbrush, clusters of spruce and pine. That he'd lived here all these months and survived soothed him. This mess of forest had saved him so far, had been his barrier to the rest of the world. He knew Michael could easily lose his way here.

Dean clapped his gloved hands together to keep warm, silently urging Eugenie to take Michael back to the house. But Michael was distracted by two crows arguing in the trees and seemed in no hurry to move on. And this moment with them standing in the woods reminded Dean of cold, aimless mornings with his unit, a forced camaraderie as they ate or smoked or just stood and stared out into the bleak landscape waiting for the next thing to happen, for orders to swoop down on them, each of them wondering whether the day would bring more than they could handle, or whether they would just be worn down by another day of tedium.

"We've just been talking," Michael said, still watching the birds squabbling in the trees. "With Ivy and the baby here, we're seeing how small the kitchen is. We'd like to add a pantry, and an extra room off the kitchen." Michael shrugged his jacket in closer around his neck. "We'd like you to do the renovation."

Dean gave a nod, shrugged a yes.

"Good. We'd better get back," Michael said to Eugenie.

Dean caught Eugenie's eye, but she quickly looked away. Listening to Michael talk, he kept to himself that he and Eugenie had already made these same plans for an addition.

∾

The baby's cries woke Eugenie. Feeling that she was still in a dream, she turned to find Michael gone. She'd conjured his homecoming; he was still in Spain and she was still alone, with Dean and Ivy and the baby. She lay in bed listening to Alice's protests and Ivy's attempts to soothe her.

She flung back the covers, pulled on a sweater and, before going down to the kitchen, looked out the window for the trail of smoke from Dean's cabin. This search for smoke had become her morning ritual, connecting her to Dean, a confirmation that all was calm in that grey spiral rising from the trees.

Downstairs, signs of Michael were everywhere. Coffee grains on the counter, the bread crumbs on the cutting board, a cupboard door wide open. She glanced out to the workshop, listening for the noise of Michael's tools. It occurred to her that he might not be there after all, that he'd gone off on one of his walks. She imagined him coming across Dean's camp.

She went to the window, thinking she ought to go warn Dean. She scoured the landscape, a farm of fallow fields. She didn't want to be on constant watch, consumed by a bitterness that seemed her own private war, unable to see how much of her life was defined by paranoia or the actions of others. Like her grandmother Eugenie needed to make the homestead work. She needed to keep things from falling apart.

Then she saw Michael emerge from the path that led to Dean's camp and she went out to him, clasping her mug of tea.

"Where'd you go?" she asked.

"Out," he said. "Walking."

"You should be careful out there in the cold. What if you get lost?"

"I wanted to have a look around, see the property. I'd like to take a look at the surveyor's plans. I was thinking there could be room to put in an orchard back there."

This was his attempt to seem engaged in the farm, she recognized, but it felt false and tangential to what he really wanted.

"Michael." Eugenie followed him to the porch. "I need to talk to you. Ivy said she'd like to buy the farm." She broached this as a challenge, a test to see how committed he was to the place. That it had come to this, that she felt they could not just talk about it as they used to when making plans, deflated her.

"We can't sell now." His abruptness startled her.

"I think I should have a say here."

"Of course. But you've done so much. I don't think this is the time to give it all up."

"I'm not giving up. No one said anything about giving up. I can do this. I have been doing this."

'With Dean's help."

"Yes, with Dean's help."

"Maybe after the kitchen renovation we won't need his help as much."

"Listen to you making all the decisions around here."

They walked into the house. Michael hung up his jacket and threw a log into the wood stove. She'd sensed a thin layer of accusation in their conversations the past few days. The farm had

157

made them different people. She'd found her ambition. Spain had made him taciturn, fractured in the way he dealt with things.

They heard Ivy's footsteps on the stairs.

"We'll talk about this later, Michael said. He stood at the kitchen window looking up to the sky. When Ivy appeared, he said, "I heard on the radio that there's an ice storm coming."

∾

The snow started just after midnight. It appeared fine and feathery at first, but turned sleet-like with the wind overnight. Pellets tapped at the window, waking Alice, leaving the rest of the house drifting in and out of sleep. By morning the world had turned ashen, the icy snow coated buildings and trees, and left the roads so slick no one dared leave the house.

"I'll make coffee," Eugenie offered.

Ivy was trying to latch Alice onto a breast. From upstairs they heard the floorboards creaking as Michael moved about getting ready for the day. The storm was tapering but the hours of wind and ice against the house had tried them all, and the baby seemed unable to settle. They ate breakfast and roamed from window to window, trying to read the storm. By noon it had stopped and Michael ventured outside, chipping his way to the workshop with a shovel.

As soon as Michael had gone, Eugenie went upstairs and checked for wood smoke from her bedroom window. She felt she was being discreet, but when she came back down, her sister shot her a questioning glance.

"How long are you going to keep this up?" Ivy asked when she'd finally got Alice to sleep.

"Keep what up?"

Ivy looked at her sideways. "Dean can't stay here forever."

Eugenie peered from the rim of her mug, then finished her coffee and placed the mug in the sink. "Do you think the renovation will upset Alice? It will create a lot of dust."

"Don't change the subject. Michael will figure out that something's up with you two. He's bound to with Dean here all the time. You can't keep avoiding the facts."

"What facts, Ivy? You're one to talk. Have you even let Alice's father know he's a father?"

"It's your life." Ivy shifted in her seat to put Alice in the cradle. "Do you remember Neil Ferguson? I taught his girls a few years ago. I saw him in town and mentioned that Dean had done a lot of work for you and he didn't know what I was talking about. He'd never heard of him." She poured herself a cup of tea and, after checking the weather again, sat down to the table. "And no, the renovation shouldn't bother Alice. I'm going to get back to the barn and start painting her crib and her dresser next week. I'll take her out there with me."

Eugenie was quiet. She went to the door and opened it a crack, feeling the cold sting her face, listening to the muffled sound of the wind as it sent ice pellets skittering along the porch. Branches had come down across the yard, snapped under the weight of the ice and she tried to calculate whether such a thing would happen in the woods with the trees shoved so closely together. She closed the door and reached for her sweater, worried Dean wouldn't have enough wood to keep the sauna warm. She had been so swept up in thinking through the secrecy of Dean's arrangement that it hadn't occurred to her that winter would pose the biggest risk of all.

"Why are you doing this?" Eugenie said.

"Why are you always protecting him?" Ivy said.

"I'm not protecting him. You know he'll go to jail or worse if he's found out."

"You are protecting him, Eugenie, and not for those reasons."

"I know this can't last. To be honest. I don't know if I can even call it an affair now, it feels like just a jumbled mess of complicated attachments. I don't know where to go with any of this, with Dean, with Michael. I feel responsible for all of it, but I can't see a way out."

"You're married, Eugenie. If that's how you feel, then don't have him lingering on your property. Dean's not right. He needs more help than you can give."

"You think I don't know that? I feel like I'm spinning and parts of me are flying off in all directions."

"You need to let something go, Eugenie. You can't carry on like this."

"Is that what you did with Alice's father, just let him go?"

Ivy bristled and turned away.

"I'm sorry. I shouldn't have said that. This is hard for you, I know. Alone here with Alice. But you've got Alice, and you've got me."

She was pacing the kitchen now, her eyes darting out the window as if Michael could walk in at any moment. He had begun talking about going back to Spain to finish the project he was working on, reminding her that his time here was only temporary. This is where she had landed, with one man who could stay with her if he truly wanted; another who couldn't, but wanted nothing more in the world.

Sleet froze against the sauna's window and Dean, listening to its constant rapping, knew he was too much on his own lately. He felt unmoored and a prisoner at the same time. He closed his eyes and nearly fell asleep, then shook himself awake when he realized he'd drifted into a dream he didn't want to be in. He stood, stretching his aching muscles, wishing he could take a hot bath. He finally managed to fall asleep around half-past three in the morning, slumped against the wall, his tools and supplies laid out before him on the bench. When he awoke four hours later, he cursed his sloppiness, throwing a handful of inlay fragments and a good bit of glue away. He was cold and stiff and he could find no consolation in the work he had done.

He pulled himself up and headed towards the workshop. The sun had yet to break over the horizon, and the white forest was bathed in a gloomy grey, the colour of his dreams. He strode across the farmyard and opened the workshop door, surprised to find Michael bent over the workbench. Dean had claimed this space, coming into the workshop early in the morning for months, before anyone in the house would be awake, taking what he needed. Now he felt like an intruder.

"Sorry, I'm just here to borrow a level." Dean said.

"Oh. Good morning." Michael rose from the stool and searched around the workshop as Dean muttered about getting a start on the renovations. "Here it is," Michael said handing it to him. "Actually, I could use a hand if you've got a moment." Michael passed one end of the armoire door to Dean. "Can you hold this steady for me? This my third attempt. I've got to get it right this time."

"What has you working so hard this early?" Dean ventured.

"I can't sleep. Different time zones, I suppose."

"This is quite the project."

"It's kept me awake many a night." Michael looked up at Dean as he adjusted the armoire door. "Is your arm holding out? I heard about the accident."

"It's healing. Still sore."

"These things take time," Michael said, his mind already elsewhere as he began placing the centrepiece of the design, a disc comprised of geometric shapes.

He began telling Dean about two other failed attempts and how this had followed months of trial and error. "There was a night I sat in my studio. I got so angry I slammed my fists against the table, sending a day's work flying across the floor. I left the studio and went out into the night and rather than head home I went up the hill behind the workshop. I was scrambling in the dark, pulling at twigs when I lost my footing. I had no idea where I was going, just anywhere other than my workbench. I knew I should go home and get some sleep. That's what I needed more than anything, but I kept moving until I was out of breath, until a stitch in my side finally slowed me down. The mountain air was so fresh, there was the smell of lemons from nearby trees and I just stood there catching my breath, feeling foolish for my actions."

Michael was concentrating on the disc but kept glancing to Dean, as if to be sure he was listening.

"Sometimes you just need to keep pushing to get things done," Dean said.

"Yes, I suppose that's what you've been doing here, with Eugenie," Michael said absently, not really looking up. "I get so tired sometimes, but I just can't stop. I get so exhausted, I just

162

stare into space. I have to remind myself that I'm not just making furniture. That there's so much more to it. The techniques. The wood itself, the nature of tree fibre, how it contracts and expands through the seasons but does not lengthen, and about veneers, and how they've been used since ancient Egypt. The principles of building furniture, making dovetails, mortise and tenon joints, these basics in woodcraft."

Dean was listening but unable to figure out what Michael was trying to say to him. Why was he telling him this? Was there some message he was trying to convey? His philosophy was crawling into Dean's mind. He started to feel agitated, the room suddenly too hot for him. He could only mutter, "A man is his work."

Michael looked up at him. "Yes, I suppose that's true." He glanced around the room and continued. "This is who I am, all I'll ever be."

When Michael finally finished what he wanted done and had inspected it with pleasure, Dean took a few steps to the door, no longer wanting to listen to Michael.

"Say, there's something I wanted to ask you about Eugenie." Michael set the armoire door down on the workbench. "Has she been okay here on her own?"

"Yes." Dean's voice was steady. "I think she's been fine."

"It's hard to tell sometimes. Long distance, the telephone. I think she's been a bit edgy with Ivy around. In any case, she doesn't seem herself."

"It's a big, never-ending job, this farm," said Dean, careful not to sound as if he was defending Eugenie any more than a hired hand would an employer. "She's been at it for a long time."

"You know, there was a time when artists like me were similar to modern day workers like you. We were paid for our painting or sculpting or what have you by the square footage rather than for the quality of the art."

Dean thought about this, about the value of the work he was doing, and that of Michael, and wondered about what his work in the military was worth. It was hard to draw conclusions, putting a price tag on a life's work like that. "How're you liking farm life then?"

"I'll be glad when the work on the house is done," Michael said, looking outside to the snow-swept fields. "Eugenie seems to think there's an endless list of things that needs to be done, but looking around I'd say she's almost there. Once the renovation is over, you can be off to your next job. Things will settle down then."

"Once the renovation is done, the rest is small stuff. I think Eugenie can handle things on her own," Dean heard himself agree. It was hard to read Michael, hard to know whether he was invested in anything he was saying, or simply distracted from his work.

"I met Jack the other day in town," Michael said. "Eugenie introduced us."

"Jack? Jack Butler?"

"Yes. Him. He said the ice storm took down hydro lines and was responsible for a three-car accident just outside of town. He said it tore part of the roof off the hunting camp. He and his friends discovered it when they went back for a bonfire with friends."

"That must have been a nasty surprise."

"I mentioned the bonfire and now Ivy wants to have one. Say, you mentioned that you're staying at your uncle's camp," Michael said. "It seems a popular thing, these camps."

Dean nodded. "They used to be a base for men when they'd go hunting. Now it's mostly a reason to get back into the woods."

"I told Jack you were living there. He was curious about the location of your uncle's camp. He said he'd been on every square mile of back roads in these parts and had a mental map of all the hunting camps in the region."

"My uncle hasn't used it in years."

"Jack also said that you should go see him if you need more work, if you're planning to stick around."

Outside, the sun began to rise over the snow-capped trees. The morning light began to creep in through the workshop windows, over to where they stood. Dean wanted to escape this conversation, and the arrival of the sun seemed the best reason for him to slip away.

∾

A bold-faced moon shone so luminous over the field it seemed like a floodlight, reminding Eugenie why they'd agreed to move here. There had been brilliant stars elsewhere of course. From that village in Spain, perched at the side of the mountain, a house that backed into a cave, where they'd sit and pick out the Belt of Orion, the Big Dipper, marvelling that these same stars had followed them from England. Nights on the terraced landscape, listening to the whoosh of water released from the irrigation system. They thought they owned the night then. Sitting, watching and listening. Waiting for inspiration, waiting to get started. This was before Antonio and marquetry and the homestead. It was all temporary back then. A few weeks when Michael would spend days carving in a nearby shed, the front doors open so that he could see the Sierra Nevada, snow-capped even in the long stifling summer. He was trying to find a way to say who he was, not a carpenter, not a woodcarver, not a furniture maker, because back then he couldn't commit to anything.

Eugenie was thinking of those days as she sat stargazing on her own. Wrapped up in her down jacket, sitting on a bench out in the front yard she waited until the cold evening chill reached through, nudging her from her post. She wandered around the yard, the light of Michael's workshop faint against the dominant moon. The crunch of snow underfoot kept a steady rhythm as she looped around the property. Michael had gone to his workshop after dinner; something needed his attention. Eugenie, wishing to avoid Ivy, told her that she was going out to see what he was working on. Instead, she wandered the yard, circling round to keep warm, searching for constellations.

The door of the workshop opened and Michael stepped out. He looked at Eugenie, surprised by the sight of her standing on her own like that.

"What are you up to?" he asked.

"Stargazing."

Michael went over to her. "A good night for celestial navigation."

"To be at sea, on a night like tonight, yes, it's a good night for watching the sky."

They walked a loop in silence, heads tilting upwards as they tried to identify constellations.

"When are you going back?" she asked.

He stopped, turned to look at her, then continued on. "In a few weeks, maybe a month. I'll stay as long as I can."

"And then what?"

"We can live in two places."

"You can."

"We can."

"But what would I do?"

"Do?"

"There's nothing for me in Spain. You know that."

"You could stay here then. We could make it work if you were to come out when I'm there, and I would be here for half the year." He was staring at her, as though challenging her to see the brilliance of his plan, even though she knew it was desperation he felt.

"How can we be together if we're apart?" she asked, knowing he had no answer for her. "I don't think we can make this work." Michael turned to her, a look of confusion across her face, then he waved his hand as if to dismiss any interpretation of what she might be telling him.

"Things would be so different if you hadn't met Antonio," Eugenie said.

This was his near miss, a diversion from the life they might have had if he had not wandered into Antonio's workshop three years ago. He'd come back that day full of excitement at the craftsmanship, the beauty of the designs. He heard the word *taracea* for the first time—Latin for *intarsia*, which means inlay. He wanted to know everything about it, the process, the materials, the designs, and so he forced himself onto Antonio as an apprentice.

"You can't really work here, can you?" Eugenie said.

"I'm doing the best I can," he said after a brief pause.

Eugenie knew this was true, that this was the best he could do. That he had tried and was only really tinkering away at his work, thoughts always back in Spain, on his real projects.

"Did Ivy tell you she's planning a bonfire for next weekend?" said Eugenie.

"She mentioned it, I didn't realize it was going ahead," he said.

"I don't think it's such a good idea. I still feel like we're strangers around here. Who is she going to invite? What is she going to tell them about us, about Dean?"

"Why would we invite Dean?"

Eugenie looked at him to see if she could read his face but it fell into the shadows.

"I guess it's Ivy's party. She can invite who she wants."

∾

Dean heard the screams and ran. Through an alley, a street, something long and narrow that he could barely see. The blackness like a fog, textured. Somehow he felt he'd been here before. He stumbled, his legs like a marionette, barely in his control. He was panicking now, trying to fight his way out, trying to escape the shouting. But it was getting louder and his legs were getting weaker…

Dean thrashed around until he got hold of his sweater, stuffing a handful in his mouth to stop his screams. He lay there, his body spent, his breath sputtering until he could see where he was, until he could see the pine boards of the sauna and realized he was safe.

After a time he drifted off only to awake again, long before the threat of frostbite that woke him most mornings now. It was the helicopters this time. Like hungry locusts they came at him, circling, soaring, lower, lower…

He jumped out of the sauna shivering in the middle of his camp, clutching the stick he'd fashioned as a club against bears. Only this time he was holding it so that it felt like his AK-14. Somewhere deep inside he was aware he was having another episode. He was so sure it was the cold metal of his gun in his hand that he stared at the club for a very long time before finally letting it fall to the ground.

The woods were a strange place to wake up after a nightmare. The trees, which should have been a tonic, merely added another layer of torture. There were monsters in the darkness that settled among the branches. The shadows, the creaking, the rustle, the looming whiteness, all worked to conjure rebels, men with guns, boys with knives, a grenade lobbed towards him. He sat crouched against a trunk, his sleeping bag wrapped around his shoulders, smoking one cigarette after another.

At long last dawn arrived. He stumbled back into the sauna, curled up against a wall and began reading *The Iliad*, skimming over the brutal war scenes. He settled on the story of Hector's wife, Andromache. She'd begged Hektor to stay, knowing that if he left she would become a widow, his son an orphan. Hector reached for his son, holding him for the last time, his wife weeping by his side. His son, startled by the gleaming bronze helmet, began to cry and Hector removed it, embraced his wife and child then went off to battle to face an outcome the gods had already determined.

Dean put the book down, his eyes blurry, recalling the day he left for Iraq. Soldiers hugging wives, husbands, or parents, fearing this would be the last they'd see of him or her, all of them carrying the weight of that thought, the knowledge that some would die. This made some of the soldiers sombre, others giddy, most of them eager to fight as they raced headlong onto the plane as if that too were some sort of battle they were rushing to.

Dean picked up the book again and, hands shaking, read of the battle that set Hector against Patroclus, who was disguised in the armour of his friend, Achilles. It was the battle that led to the killing of Patroclus, who was no match for Hector and whose death would bring Achilles back into battle, seeking revenge. The gods had set it up; Hector must die.

That was the story of war, Dean knew. To keep the killing cycle going until someone decides it's over, because the loss of human lives, would never be enough to end it.

Dean lit a match and watched the trail of smoke spiral above him. He was still in his bunk, having spent the bulk of his day there, unwilling to move. He held the flame over his palm, counting to see how long he could hold it before the pain got too much… six, seven, eight, nine…

∽

The day before the bonfire, a dense frozen fog swept in. The trees, the barn, the telephone poles all disappeared into the milky ceiling while fists of clouds settled into bushes and floated in the lower fields. Forecasters remarked on the sudden warming and promised a clearing later in the day but the atmosphere, like Eugenie's mood, remained sombre. Ivy had already left for town, Michael was in his workshop and Dean had not yet appeared. The fog gave a dreamy quality to the homestead, everything shrouded, with blurred edges, and it frightened her, to have so much obscured.

She glanced at the workshop where Michael was immersed

in a new design, then snuck past to the path, its track now etched into their property. Reaching the camp, she touched the kettle on the propane burner. Still warm.

"Dean," she whispered, wondering if he'd fallen asleep. She went to the other side of the sauna and saw a board laid flat out like a bench on top of two stumps. On the ground there was a tray containing glue and a few woodworking tools. Edging closer she saw that the board had an abstract form of marquetry, a design that looked like mountains. Or waves. She knelt beside it, touching it, following the undulating form with her fingertips.

The crunch of snapped twigs announced Dean's return and Eugenie turned around to see him approach swinging two rabbits on a string.

"I wasn't expecting you," he said as he set the rabbits down.

"I came to let you know that things at the house have grown complicated. There's the bonfire tonight. It might be best if you stayed away."

"I don't think I'm up for a party anyways." He wiped his hands on his jacket.

"Neil Ferguson will be there." She was looking at him, willing him to confess. "You never worked for Neil did you?"

"No."

"Then why lie about it?"

"I needed a job. I saw his name on the mailbox and figured the mention of his name was as good as a reference. I didn't have a choice."

"You could have told me. Later."

"You get stuck in a lie, it's hard to crawl back out."

"Are there any other lies you're stuck in?"

He took his knife out and began cutting the rope from the

rabbits' feet. He took his cigarettes from his pocket and threw it to Eugenie after putting one between his lips. She fumbled with the pack, pulled the matches out and set it down, deciding against following his lead.

"I didn't know you then."

Dean squinted as the smoke rose to his face while he held one of the rabbits in position to begin skinning it. Eugenie looked away from Dean, not wanting to watch. He had become an expert, completing both in less than twenty minutes.

"I want you to find a solution," she said. "I don't want you to live like this. You have to do things differently. You can't keep hiding. Someone will end up hurt."

Dean stared in a way that seemed to be looking through her. She'd started to see this now that she was looking, his ability to disappear into himself, into some place that had nothing to do with her. She noticed the tremor in his hand and she reached out to quiet it. Her touch startled him and he pulled away from her, his look of fear frightening her.

"No." His voice was too loud for the silence of the forest and it echoed among the trees.

"Turning yourself in is the only way out of this. I've been reading about soldiers who went back and ended up with a discharge, not punishment. If you can return to your base, get discharged, then you can come back to Canada legally."

"They got lucky," Dean said.

"It's not just luck. The military doesn't want to spend their resources on deserters."

"That's not their official line. Those soldiers got lucky. I know how the military works. This unofficial policy could change at any minute, or at the whim of a commanding officer."

172

"It could be a chance worth taking."

The sun ripped through the clouds, its sudden light jarring. Then in an instant the sun was gone. Dean stood and turned to her. She started to speak but he kissed her words silent.

"Maybe we should just run away. We could do it, you know. Run away and be happy," Dean said, frustrated. "When Michael leaves for Spain, I'll make some phone calls. I can't promise anything, but I'll do that much at least. In the spring, we'll plant the orchard. That field behind the barn, we can get rid of the rusting farm equipment and put in more apple trees."

"I'm trying to do what's best," she said. She held his hand for a moment. "I have to get back."

∾

Which direction does the tab on the army belt extend to on the male Class A uniform? *The wearer's left.* Why is the flag worn on the right shoulder of the Utility Uniform? *The flag is worn on the right shoulder to give the effect of the flag flying in the breeze as the wearer moves forward.* Where do you walk when walking with someone that is senior to you? *On the senior person's left.* What is the official song of the US Army? *"The Army Goes Rolling Along."* How many Norths are there on a military map? *Three: True north, Magnetic north, Grid north.* Which means of communication is least secure? *Radio.* Which means of communication is most secure? *Messenger.* If you sleep on duty, what could your punishment be? *Court Martial.*

There was a lot Dean knew. He knew the weight of the M4 rifle (6.49 pounds). He knew the velocity (2970 ft per second), the range (3924 yards). He knew the most important requirement in a survival situation (water) and he knew that according

to the Geneva Convention the only information POWs were re-
quired to give was name, rank, age and service number.

This was his new morning routine. Reciting military facts.
Then, as he'd done this morning, he would march the army
standard fifteen-inch step down to the stream. It was an exercise to focus his mind, to think by rote of what he knew, rather
than of what was going on at the moment.

Dean was going through this routine in the barn, as he was
preparing some timber from the loft he wanted to reclaim for
shelving in the new kitchen. It would help with costs, he'd agreed
with Eugenie, and make the renovation in keeping with the house.
He would slice the boards into planks for shelves and joists to be
ready for when the weather allowed construction to begin.

He moved a container of turpentine off the table then went
back to working on the planks, his thoughts turning to a conversation he'd overheard Eugenie and Michael having the night
before. They thought they were alone in the yard looking up
the stars, but he had been crouching nearby in field. It amazed
him how little of his presence they could sense in the dark. Michael didn't want to stay; Eugenie didn't want to go. If he could
stretch out the kitchen project long enough, Dean thought,
then he could find a way to stay.

He was calculating how long that might take when Ivy
walked into the barn. Ivy had been in the barn every day this
week restoring furniture, and doing a bad job of it from what
Dean could see. They'd been forced to share the space these past
days, but wherever possible he'd kept his distance. Dean felt her
presence around him like a dark cloud, her every move and
utterance weighted with judgement. Eugenie had assured him
that Ivy had her own issues to deal with, but it seemed to him

that Ivy was biding her time too, waiting for the right moment to reveal her true nature.

Ivy started humming. Her arm was at an awkward angle as she painted a child's rocking chair and she seemed lost in a melody that kept her focussed on her work. Dean was finding it hard to concentrate. He cleared his throat to interrupt her, to jar her out of it, but she didn't seem to notice.

"I'm having some people by tomorrow evening, for a bonfire," Ivy finally said, not looking up from her work. "You can come, if you like."

"I'll keep that in mind."

"It might be awkward for you with Michael there, but there will be others. Neil Ferguson and his wife. You know Neil, right? Eugenie said you once worked for him."

Dean felt there was something more she wanted to say. "Sure, I know Neil."

She started sanding spindles of the rocking chair that were crusted with old paint.

"I ran into Neil in town the other day, and we got to talking after I invited him and his wife. Funny thing he said. He doesn't remember you at all."

Dean began using the electric sander, ignoring Ivy's comment, an attack really, as the grinding noise filled the barn for the next ten minutes. When he turned it off he could hear Ivy humming again. He'd gotten used to it, this humming, but today, something switched in him, and the notes became something of a message, a signal that she was trying to send, and he immediately thought she was transmitting a code. Dean felt a tightening in his chest, his hand shaking as he saw the figure in the corner of the room. There was something not right, the sound of her humming was now a warning, a sound that shouldn't be there, in the room late at night like this; there were insurgents in the area, and this was her signal, calling them, giving their position away. He dived over to her, desperate to stop her, his hand clasped against her mouth, but not before she let out a scream as he knocked her back against the wall. He was in a frenzy, looking around for the enemy to storm in. He felt her push against him, trying to get his hands off her mouth, he felt her bite him but he held on, struggling to get control of the situation. He was in close now, his head against hers, telling her to be quiet.

He could see the inside of the house, a dim room that held a table with glasses of tea, a swirl of mats on the floor, pictures hung slanted on the wall. Dean had led the platoon through the dark hallway, checking doors, working their way through the rooms. A shot out back had lured them down the hall as though a trap had been set for them. Another shot came from somewhere in the darkness. When they burst through the back door, the soldiers followed Dean to the cloistered yard with vines hanging overhead, making the place seem sinister in the darkness. Then came another shot and this one they took as an attack so he opened fire. The other soldiers followed.

There were twenty seconds of fire. That's how long it took to kill the mother, the grandfather and the teenage boy. The father was injured, crouched in the corner clutching a small knife, already he was weeping though he couldn't have known who had been killed; the darkness held the secrets that would destroy his life. It was the grandmother who was humming, holding her grandson in her arms as if soothing him to sleep.

Dean felt someone pull him away. He saw Michael press him against the barn post and was unable to understand what was happening. He saw Eugenie's face in the barn doorway, a look he didn't recognize and he reached for her but she was too far away. He wanted to speak but all the words seemed trapped in his head. He took a long deep breath and closed his eyes.

Ivy staggered away from him in tears, her sweater torn, her lip bleeding.

"I killed them," he muttered. "I killed them," he said again and again. The house full of insurgents was gone, the soldiers, the people he'd killed all disappeared leaving him with a truth he wished he'd never uncovered.

∾

Eugenie thought back to those months before Dean showed up, when she was alone in the house, how she'd chipped away at a list of tasks she'd set for herself. The overriding memory of that time was of fear. Not of living alone, but of being alone. She'd moved to England as a young woman because she saw what being alone had done to her grandmother, who'd become bitter, angry at a world that had taken away her husband and then her daughter and son-in-law. Eugenie had grown up learning to tamp down her feelings. Now she feared she was unable to distinguish one emotion from the other.

Solitude can be disorienting, loneliness blinding. She had seen in Dean what she had wanted to see, but now it was obvious that there was much more to him than she could manage. He was troubled. Convincing Ivy he wasn't dangerous was futile. Looking across the kitchen table now at Ivy, pressing an ice pack to her lip, Eugenie realized there was a brittleness that defined her sister—her demanding ways, her forceful interrogations, the manner in which she occupied any space she entered. This had been the price Ivy had paid for losing parents so young.

"You've put our lives in danger," Ivy said. "That man is capable of killing us all."

"He's a war resister, not a killer. He's sick."

"He's delusional and trained to kill. My God, there's a baby in this house."

"Let's just go easy, Ivy." Eugenie folded her arms and leaned against the kitchen counter. "It could have just as easily been me he grabbed. Dean didn't even see you. Don't you realize that? He just got back from Iraq. It's got nothing to do with you."

"It doesn't matter that he didn't know what he was doing. He could have *killed* me."

"I don't think it would have gone that far. He had a breakdown, Ivy. I know this has been tough. I know you were hurt. I'm sorry for that. I didn't see this coming. I never imagined him as a threat."

Ivy stared at Eugenie. "He could have killed me." She was whimpering now and Eugenie went to her. She held her awkwardly, thinking how uncomfortable they were in each other's arms. They stayed that way for a while, talking about how it was that the two of them were back at their grandmother's house after so many years, and how violence seemed to follow them there, and that perhaps the place really was cursed.

"What happened to you in Japan, Ivy?"

"I fell in love."

"At what price? Love is not supposed to make you lose your way."

"No, but it's hard to control, it's not supposed to have a price. Has love made you lose your way?"

Eugenie wanted to say that she was not in love with Dean, but she realized that she couldn't be sure it would sound convincing coming out of her mouth. Instead, she watched Ivy go to Alice who had started fussing in the bassinet. The tenderness with which she handled her daughter was startling. Eugenie wondered if this form of love, so even-handed and reliable, had been bestowed upon her sister with the birth.

They had lost so much, the two of them, when their parents died. They had to figure out so much on their own, about life, and about love. Neither of them had been good at it. Seeing Ivy with Alice, Eugenie understood she still had much to learn; grappling with her emotions was never going to be easy.

∽

Dean thought he could hear voices, but knew he was too far away. He'd been watching the embers fade to grey, poking the ashes with a stick until the bones from the rabbit were buried. He didn't like cooking the rabbits late in the day like this; he figured it was an invitation to the coyotes, the raccoons, even the bears that he knew tramped nearby.

He walked around his camp, listening for voices and pretending not to. He'd told Eugenie he would stay clear of the party, but now he was working himself into some sort of mood, a restlessness drawing him in. He prowled the campsite thinking that maybe he could go, have a beer, see the way Eugenie was with Michael.

Dean realized he was circling his camp like an animal, protecting his territory; something was on his mind and he couldn't quite work it out. He was thinking of those last days in Iraq, waiting to leave. A time when it seemed they were all on edge. After months of expecting the next attack or following yet another command that might put them in danger, the days of waiting to go home became the toughest. No one had any fight left in him. All the nerve, adrenaline, courage or fear that had sent them running headlong into battle seemed a crazy drug they'd taken that had now worn off. The curse of getting killed days before going home hung over them, though they pretended otherwise. They cleaned their guns and played cards or video games or watched movies or just sat and picked up pieces of conversations they'd heard or told a hundred times already. Dean spent a good deal of time wondering what came next after his leave. He'd already gotten notice of his redeployment, but even then he knew he wouldn't be going back.

Then the last battle came. Shots in the nearby town, one soldier down. They suited up, their gear already feeling like something out of their past, and headed out. Dean remembered the moment of driving down the dirt road, the sunset like the blue of the ocean near his home in Maine and everyone so silent it might have been a Sunday drive.

He threw the dregs of his coffee on top of the ashes and started walking towards the party, still thinking about that drive because it seemed that his tour of duty ended on that dirt road. The stink of garbage and that blue horizon became etched in his mind because he couldn't remember anything beyond that point, which he figured was a good place to end the war. Sometimes the details could mess with your head.

At the bonfire, the flames were shooting for the moon, sparks fluttering, then floating like dreamy fireflies before disappearing into the darkness. The night was cold but dry, and Dean looked to the fire with longing. Standing in the bushes, his hand cupping the last of his cigarette, he pulled his jacket in tighter, put on his woollen toque and watched. He saw Ivy talking to someone he didn't recognize, Michael sitting in a chair, Eugenie nearby, while two others were just arriving. He saw Jack, who was standing back away from the fire.

The effect was mesmerizing: the orange glow of the fire, the banter, the tender ease of a mid-winter gathering. Dean crouched against a tree, watching as the man he now knew was Neil Ferguson arrived with his wife, Catherine, the circle around the fire widening to let them in. Ivy was talking to Neil and his wife about when she'd taught their daughters in school, but Dean wasn't paying attention to the conversation. He was concentrating on the large pile of burning logs that pulsed red. This pulsing, like a heartbeat, transfixed Dean, as if it were a living, breathing thing. With the logs piled vertically, the bonfire began to resemble a pyre and Dean had a flash image of a figure made of twisted straw, with flames shooting in every direction. A wicker man.

Dean shuddered and looked away from the fire. Too many sleepless nights made him feel dizzy, disoriented. After a moment he looked back, soon drawn into the pulsing again, imagining he could feel the feverish heat, thinking of the image, the wicker man that kept playing through his mind. A fragment emerged, a scene from a movie he'd seen, a wicker man constructed to represent a human burned at the stake. A sacrifice to the gods. Only in the movie it was a man burning inside the wicker structure.

He was jolted from this grotesque vision by laughter, a high squeal he recognized as coming from Ivy, and then Eugenie said something that made them laugh even harder. He realized he'd missed the joke, and a small part of him thought they were

181

laughing at him. He pushed against this, sure that his paranoia was getting the better of him.

He looked over to Eugenie, who was now talking to Jack. He wished she would come to him and take him back to his camp. They could build their own fire. It would be quieter there with just the two of them.

The fire collapsed as the logs underneath burned to ash, and Michael rose from his seat to pile more on top. Dean could hear Michael telling Neil's wife about his work in Spain and hearing his voice from this distance, soft and earnest, Dean was mesmerized; it was a far cry from the voices he'd been listening to over the past few years—barking orders, shouting salutations, raucous laughing, fucking this, fucking that. There seemed no volume other than loud, crazed, or chaotic. He'd forgotten how much he hated it.

Dean was drifting in and out of the conversation, pulled away by memories of those cold nights back with his unit, with oil barrel fires to keep them warm when they could be bothered, nights filled with jokes, tales of sexual adventures, boasts, and taunts, the stories young men tell to amuse and to escalate their standing.

He shook himself from this memory when he heard Ivy humming near the path where he hid. She was getting closer and he crouched stone still, waiting to be discovered, but she was only gathering more wood for the fire from the granary. He heard her rustling around inside the building, the rhythm of her voice seeping through the thin outer walls so that he began to feel that she could see through them, that she could see him on the other side. He held his breath, and tracked her movements until she'd left the building and went back to the fire.

Dean knew it was time to go back to his camp. He watched as Eugenie dropped her sausage and busied herself with poking it into the ashes, thinking that if he could just walk out there, past her husband, and sister and newfound friends, if he could just go up and kiss her in front of everyone, everything would be okay.

Instead, he turned and walked into the woods.

∾

Standing around the bonfire, Eugenie could sense Dean's presence in the bush behind the treeline. She wanted to go to him, quietly take him back to his camp but didn't dare. He could be in the midst of another episode, for all she knew. With everyone there, who knew what kind of scene he was capable of making. She knew he would have to leave the farm now, that things had fallen apart in ways she hadn't imagined. The part of him that was broken, the part that he'd concealed from her, had finally crept ahead. She had to tell him, but she had no idea how he would take it, and that scared her. She'd seen signs of his imbalance, she now admitted to herself, but it was the man who listened to her life story without judgement, who created a refuge in the forest, who had dreams for the farm as big as hers, who listened to her and consoled her when she needed it, that she got to know. Or wanted to know.

It was hard to defend him after he attacked Ivy. She closed her eyes and saw the memory of it. Ivy shouting, Michael pulling him away from her. The order to get off the property, a frenzied demand to call the police. It had gotten out of hand so quickly that Eugenie had arrived on the scene almost as it was over. Then came the apologies. I'm sorry, I'm sorry, I'm sorry…over and over, so thorough and emphatic they were unsure whether he was apologizing to them or to those he had harmed in war.

She'd calmed Ivy down, persuaded Michael that calling the police would only make things worse. She would take care of things, she told them, but neither was convinced. "I'll tell him he has to leave. I'll tell him he needs to get help, that there is nothing we can do for him, that he needs professional help."

Perhaps Jack could help, she thought, watching him crack jokes around the fire. Jack had been through this, the weight of war. He would know what to do. Michael had told her about meeting up with him in town, the offer of work for Dean, as though they could pass him along like some farm implement.

She would speak to Dean tomorrow. It was better this way, rather than have Michael take over as he'd planned, telling Eugenie that he would go tell Dean he couldn't work there anymore. She didn't need more of Michael stomping around, telling Eugenie that he knew something like this would happen.

Eugenie was so tired from it all. The next morning she stood alone in the kitchen, thinking about what she needed to do. Ivy was still upstairs with Alice, and Michael was back in his workshop. The day was rolling up, in an hour the sun would be over the trees. She saw the trail of smoke against the grey sky. If she left now, she could be back before anyone could notice.

When she reached the camp, though, it looked withered. Inside the sauna, she came upon Dean fast asleep. She crept around, quietly putting a log in the stove. Eugenie wished she could contain this moment, the suspension of any discussion or decision, a badly needed respite. There'd been too much to consider lately, too much to take on and she felt an inner tremor as though things might continue to unspool to the point where she couldn't contain it any longer.

This was her fear, to have everything out of control with nowhere to latch onto; to be alone, all over again.

She sat watching him, wanting to wake him so she could see which version would be there, as if the two sides were interchangeable. She had to shoulder some of the blame, she now realized. She'd taken him in, fallen in love, assumed he was as he'd presented himself and not someone with baggage or a backstory. It was hard to think about what Dean could have done to her, or to Alice, or to any one of them. Now that it had happened once, she wondered, how long it would remain just below the surface, waiting for the one thing that would set him off again.

She ran all the way back to the house.

ॐ

Dean woke up in a panic, to the sound of feet scurrying away from his camp. He was being watched. He picked up his knife and rushed outside, but no one was there. Agitated, he sat down on a log, picked up a piece of wood that lay at his feet and furiously scraped away the bark, rotating the branch until he'd reached the bony inside.

He ran his hand over the knots, picking at the hair-like fringes, trying to keep his night thoughts away. Last night it was a woman with her son, her body draped in black. She was scolding him while holding onto his upper arm so that he couldn't escape, issuing words of love and worry, and the boy looked worried too, but not in the way of his mother. His worry was one of punishment, of treats withheld, a curfew enforced. Her worry was of death.

Dean ran the blade over the wood, smoothing the bumps, the chips falling to his feet, scattering across his boots. The boy from his dreams, standing in the shadow of his mother, had wrangled free for a moment, poised to run off again but her hand reached for his shirt and pulled him back, half embracing, half protecting. Then the mother was jolted forward, still clutching her child, one hand reaching for a knife wound in her abdomen that suddenly appeared. She fell to her knees, her hand sliding off her son's, dropping to the silky dirt. It was her falling that kept playing in his mind, her hand slapping against the dirt, over and over again, a continuous loop from which he couldn't break free.

Dean laid his knife down beside him. He stayed in the sauna most of the day, expecting Eugenie to come and tell him the consequences of his actions, but that never happened. Now that night was upon him again, he was wide awake. He wished Eugenie were here with him. His insides felt gouged, his body limp. He felt great pains in his chest. At times he thought he was dying. This pain, like when Nick was killed, wore at him because he'd thought he wasn't capable of any emotion that might tear him down again. He wanted to get back to that place where he felt nothing at all, where no one could touch him.

He held the piece of wood out in front of him, examining his work. It was hard to say what it was, what it could be. He'd started it without a plan, just manically peeling it apart. Still, it had a promising shape to it. Perhaps he could fashion a pipe from it, or a bird. A bird would be nice.

Knife in hand, Dean went to the barn before dawn because no one had told him he couldn't. In the barn, he sanded the planks as if nothing had happened, thinking of the flaw that held him hostage, a weakness that was insidious and slippery. Achilles had a vulnerability too, and it had cost him his life. Achilles was shot by a poisonous arrow in the ankle, his weak point, the one place that his mother had not been able to protect when she'd bathed him in sacred water. Dean wondered if he'd hit upon his own weak point, this inability to disconnect what he'd been through with how he needed to live, to break through to the other side of it, where it could just be a memory and not something that afflicted him, something that no longer lived inside him.

Trying to piece together that night in Iraq felt like links in a chain that had no order to it. He remembered the call. The co-ordinates took him to a suspected safe house for insurgents. He stood at its threshold, his men leaning back against the outside wall, waiting to go in. It was his decision to lead his men into battle. He kept thinking of what his commanding officer would have done, of how he could have done it differently. He'd followed a rational plan, a logical train of thought that led him to where he was now.

He leaned against the wall in the barn and lit a cigarette. He listened for voices but heard nothing. The place was so quiet he wondered whether they might have left without him knowing. His heart ached for Eugenie but he couldn't go to her now. He stubbed his cigarette out and closed his eyes, feeling that sleep was not far off. He was afraid to let himself go, worried about what would reappear in his dreams.

He heard a car pull into the driveway. Looking out the window, Dean saw a police car approaching the yard. He saw the lights go on in the house and knew it wouldn't be long before they hunted him down. Ignoring the pain in his body, he ran to the woods and scampered over the crest of the hill, twigs beating against his shirt. Leaping over a log, he beat away the bush as it thickened around him. He would get out of here; he would break free and sprint through the woods until he was safe.

The trees roared past him and he pushed himself to run faster, harder, the burning in his chest a reminder that he was a soldier, able to withstand physical duress not known to civilians. His arms propelling him forward, his legs flying over forest debris in a rush of euphoria as he palpitated with freedom.

But then Dean caught sight of an animal, a squirrel, a fox, something moving ahead of him, a distraction that threw him off his stride, and that was enough. A tree branch long dead, now covered in ice, lay in his path. His foot slid forward, twisting his ankle as he went down.

He struggled to get up, his breath ragged as he gulped for air, but a sharp pain in his ankle kept him down. Stumbling, he tried again, half-hobbling, half-running into the wilderness. The heat of his body quickly dissipated, his sweat now giving him a chill. He shook the snow from his hands and clapped them together to rustle some warmth. His foot seared with pain at each step. He clasped at tree trunks, branches, anything that might ease the pain. Everything slowed, the air, his breath, his steps. He heard the crack and snap of breaking twigs everywhere. He wiped his forehead with the back of one hand and felt only cold sweat on his skin. He found a stick to use as a cane, and stumbled when it cracked in two, hurling him forward into a mound of snow. He lay there, imagining Eugenie calling for him, the sound of her voice floating about the trees. His breathing slowed. Time stood still. He was relieved to have a moment's rest. All he needed was a few minutes to get his strength. He began to feel warm again. He stared at the mesh of trees hovering over him, at the sun that sent streaks of light that he was sure pointed to his position. Eugenie would be there soon, he knew. And he would be waiting for her.

∾

When she saw the police car pull up the lane, Eugenie turned to Ivy. "What have you done?"

"Nothing. I haven't done anything," Ivy was looking out the window at the officer walking to the house.

"I called them," said Michael, coming down the stairs. "When I went out this morning, I found him in my workshop with a knife in his hand. Don't you get that he's lost it, Eugenie? Does someone have to die for you to realize?"

"I won't forgive you for this," Eugenie said as she grabbed her coat and went outside.

Michael followed her. "Thanks for coming, officer."

"I saw someone run into the woods," said the officer. "Is that your man?"

"That's him," said Michael, taking charge. "His name is Dean. He's an American deserter who's been squatting on our property. He's not stable."

The officer looked out at the expanse of white trees. "Do you know where he lives?"

Michael looked back at Eugenie. "My wife does."

She knew then that, though he'd never admit it, Michael had always suspected her relationship with Dean. This was his way of letting her know. By removing Dean from the farm, Michael was ending the affair for her.

"Ma'am, can you please lead the way?"

The cold morning air stung her face and she felt a burning in her chest as she led them through the woods. She looked through the trees for signs of smoke but the air was clear, and when they arrived at the camp she saw the sauna door swung open, and inside the stove held no fire. Her eyes darted over his things in search of clues, but everything was intact.

"This is it," she said.

"He must be hiding deeper in the woods," said the officer. "He saw my car."

"He might have gone already," Eugenie said. "He could be miles from here."

"If he's not well and feeling cornered, he could be a danger to himself or others. I'm going to have to call this in."

Back at the house, she gave the officer a statement of Dean's appearance and listened as the officer filed his report. Dean was now officially a wanted man.

By the next morning, the police called to say they'd had no sightings of Dean in the town or along any of the main roads. Michael disappeared into his workshop again. The night before, she had asked him to leave, and he hadn't argued.

Fearing for Dean's safety, Eugenie walked back into the woods and past the sauna, taking a trail she and Dean had taken when they'd embarked on their surveying adventures. Soon she found herself at the pond, now frozen, where they'd made love, the rock where they'd whiled away summer afternoons.

They hadn't considered how things would turn out back then. It was all desire and living for the moment. A fugitive's life, she now realized. She'd thought she could fix whatever was broken with Dean, not fully registering how badly damaged he was. She should have seen the signs, she should have known that he needed her in a way she wasn't prepared for. She leaned against the rock, now encased in ice, and caught her breath, placed a hand over her thumping heart, wondering how close she was to panic.

She pressed on, trudging across the slushy shore towards another trail that took her to the tree that had fallen in the storm. Now covered in snow, the trunk of the elm tree was still sprawled across the meadow, a gouge in the landscape, the pine and spruce still adjusting to the hole it left. She walked towards it, watchful of the surrounding woods for signs of movement.

"Dean, please," she cried out of desperation. "It's Eugenie. Please come out."

The forest stood solemn, the wind still as death and Eugenie took a few steps in one direction then stopped, uncertain where to go next, her voice breaking as she called out. Nothing. She staggered, circling the open area in desperation, willing him to appear, but still there was silence. She would make one wider circle through the woods then head back in the direction of home. She'd already been gone for an hour and a half, though she had no idea of time passing. She would go back and get supplies, warmer clothes, and a map before heading out again.

Then she saw Dean. He was slumped against a tree as if sleeping, his head drooping off to the side, boughs draped over him as if to protect him from the cold.

"Dean," she shouted, running to him. She grabbed him, and started shaking him roughly, then rubbing his body as if she might revive him. She held onto his jacket, running her hand over his face, the sharp bristles of his chin familiar, so familiar it was impossible to believe that he wouldn't wake up. "Dean, it's me. I'm here. Dean, talk to me."

Over and over, she said his name, pleading with him to wake up. Then, when she was spent, when the realization of what had happened hit her, she lay next to him, her arms wrapped around him, her body heaving from the exertion. In the distance she heard her name but she ignored it. It was just the two of them, and she would never leave him. She lay there holding him, murmuring, *It's okay, it's okay* until Michael finally came to pull her away.

∾

The officers came to clear away Dean's belongings. They took his tent, his cooking supplies, the clothes that he had folded and stacked next to his sleeping bag. Then they took Dean away. His body crumpled under a covering, one boot hanging over the edge, his shoelace swinging as they carried him out of the forest.

Eugenie answered all their questions and watched the ambulance drive away. Once the police were finally satisfied, they left her alone.

Later in the day, she went back to the sauna and leaned into the wall that was now fully marked with Dean's work. She looked at the waves dotted with geometric shapes, tracing her finger along the design as if trying to read into what was on his mind, the need to commune with him through the message on the wall making her feel agitated and so full of grief she could barely breathe. She stretched her arms out across the wall, face pressed into it, trying to conjure something of Dean, but there was only the rough prickle of wood against her skin, the faint smell of adhesive. The complete erasure of him seemed more than she could bear. She clutched the wall, feeling the slats scrape her face.

She lay shivering on the bench, closed her eyes, wishing for sleep to take her away. When she finally opened her eyes she noticed the tools that were laid out on the floor, done so with the precision of a surgeon. They were Michael's tools of course, but she did not make the distinction. Next to the tools was a book, *The Iliad*. She held it to her chest as she lay on the bench, unable to move until finally dusk urged her back to the house.

∾

"He was stealing from me." Michael gripped a handful of tools, preparing them for the box that sat on his workbench.

"I know." Days had passed since Dean's death, days of protracted silence and strained small talk.

Michael was packing up his workshop. His flight to Spain was in forty-eight hours and he was struggling to get everything together.

"There was so much I didn't see." He was tying the strings of one of the pouches, slowly, as if it were an ancient art.

"Most of the time you weren't interested in anything you didn't want to look at." Eugenie turned away from him, letting his anger rest between them, not wanting to go over territory they'd already covered. "Do you remember that night in Conchur," she said finally. "You stayed in the studio almost the entire night. I came to you at dawn but you'd fallen asleep. I told you that it was too much, your work was not helping you and you muttered, half in your sleep, that it was the only thing that was helping you."

Michael looked up at her, waiting to see where she was going with this.

"That's when you left me."

"I see." He waved his hand around in front of him gesturing to his surroundings. "And this. Were we ever to make something of this?"

"Yes, that was always the dream." She took a few steps towards him. "But you never showed up. And now I have made something of it, something that's mine."

He would not look at her, instead turning back to his materials, packing them into the boxes that lined his workbench.

After, as she sat in the sauna reading *The Iliad*, she thought of the life she was supposed to have with Michael, how they'd strived to come up with a plan. This was the work of the gods, she thought, the gods who wandered around disguised as mortals but who determined the fate of those who prowl the earth. She was never meant to live here with Michael. It was why the gods had invented the war that sent Dean into something that was beyond him, why they sent him into the house in Iraq that tricked him into battle, that drove him away from the army and into her backwoods, that led him to her door. It was fate, the handiwork of the gods.

∾

Green shoots had finally begun to sprout up through the melting snow, a signal winter was finally coming to an end. Eugenie made it to the house just before the first spring rain of the year fell on the slushy grounds. She shed her wool coat and lit the gas stove to put the kettle on, then opened the shutters on the back window. The rain began with great splats on the porch and soon there was a steady thrumming on the roof. She stood in the doorway, watching it douse her garden. Soon she'd begin sowing new seeds. Ivy had promised to help; they would sow this year's harvest together.

She was glad for the rain. The winter had been so hard on her that she was glad for a symbolic end to its torment. Something to wash away the last dregs of her marriage, to settle the soil where Dean had died. As a point of remembrance, she'd kept the sauna free of encroaching spiderwebs, cut the bushes back, cleared out the fire pit. She'd raked and trimmed and gathered stones and created a form of retreat where she would go each day, sometimes just to check on it, other times to sit and read, or to think about Dean.

Eugenie placed her coffee on the table and pulled the paper and pen from her bag, and set them down. After she'd drunk her coffee, she picked up her pen.

Dear Victoria,

I knew your brother.

Eugenie stared at the paper just as she'd done each time she tried to write the letter. It was as though this too, just the starting of it, was part of a ritual in honouring Dean. *Guilt stays with you.* When did Dean tell her this? What was it they were talking about? All those conversations that now came to her in fragments, her memory piecing things together in a way that left her feeling bereft, and that's how she came to the idea of writing to his sister, thinking this would be a way of telling her all that Eugenie knew of her brother, what he'd told her about the war. But there seemed no place to start, no place to tell Dean's sister how she'd let him down, how she hadn't seen the extent of his suffering, because she was worried about the void she'd become in her own failing marriage.

She sat for some time, listening to the rain, and after it stopped she went out to the porch. She heard a car door slam. That would be Ivy home already. She was early today. Then she heard her sister calling out to her. Eugenie had forgotten that Alice had a doctor's appointment. She folded the letter she'd started and slipped it in her back pocket.

The farm had consumed her since Dean's death. In time, she would learn how to make this place thrive after so much trauma. For now, there were things she had learned about falling in love, and things she'd never imagined she was capable of doing. Dean had taught her to pay attention, to take risks, to make plans and follow them through. Spring was coming. She had to look to the future. The past was only ever something she had to leave behind.

ACKNOWLEDGEMENTS

I am immensely grateful to my editor, Dimitri Nasrallah, for his considerable support, generosity, and skill while working on *The Deserters*. My thanks also to Simon Dardick, publisher, and Derek Webster, marketing manager, and to everyone else at Véhicule Press for helping to bring the book to fruition.

A special thanks to Helen Humphreys for her astute guidance with early drafts of the novel and for suggesting its title.

There are many people who provided various forms of support during the writing of the book. In particular, I would like to thank Erin Bow, Susan Fish, Kristen Mathies, Nan Forler, Tamas Dobozy, Kim Knowles, Penelope Overton, and Susan Scott.

While working on *The Deserters* I had the great fortune to reunite with my cousin First Sergeant William Jackson. I want to thank him for his willingness to talk to me about his experiences as a soldier in the US Army during the Iraq War, especially about the topic of Post-Traumatic Stress Disorder, which helped to underscore the importance of writing about this subject.

In addition, I read many books that greatly helped my understanding of the complex issues involved in this area. Among the most useful were: *The Good Soldiers* by David Finkel; *Thank You For Your Service* by David Finkel; *The Forever War* by Dexter Filkens; *Generation Kill* by Evan Wright; *Beyond Duty* by Shannon Meehan; *War* by Sebastian Junger; and *Erratic North* by Mark Frutkin. Silas Kopf's *A Marquetry Odyssey: Historical Objects and Personal Work* was also extremely helpful in guiding me through the world of marquetry. Readers interested in more on the *Illiad* will find much to please them in *The Song of Achilles* by Madeline Miller, *The War That Killed Achilles: The True Story of Homer's Iliad and the Trojan War* by Caroline Alexander, and *The Theatre of War: What Ancient Greek Tragedies Can Teach Us Today* by Bryan Doerries.

I greatly appreciate the support of the Canada Council for the professional writer's grant during the development of *The Deserters*.

This book would not have been possible without the unfailing encouragement and support from Darren and from Esme. With love to the moon and back, I thank them both for believing that *The Deserters* would see the light of day.

ESPLANADE
Books

THE FICTION IMPRINT AT VÉHICULE PRESS

The Goddess of Fireflies : A novel by Geneviève Pettersen
[Translated from the French by Neil Smith]
All That Sang : A novella by Lydia Perović
Hungary-Hollywood Express : A novel by Éric Plamondon
[Translated from the French by Dimitri Nasrallah]
English is Not a Magic Language : A novel by Jacques Poulin
[Translated from the French by Sheila Fischman]
Tumbleweed : Stories by Josip Novakovich
A Three-Tiered Pastel Dream : Stories by Lesley Trites
Sun of a Distant Land : A novel by David Bouchet
[Translated from the French by Claire Holden Rothman]
The Original Face : A novel by Guillaume Morissette
The Bleeds : A novel by Dimitri Nasrallah
Nirliit : A novel by Juliana Léveillé-Trudel
[Translated by Anita Anand]
The Deserters : A novel by Pamela Mulloy